BEYOND THE COBWEBS

by Chayele Kohane

Trust Publications
21 Egerton Road
London N16 6UE

Cover art, layout and design: Eli Toron
Editor: Yael Lock

Printing and binding:

Distributed by:

Israel Bookshop
Judaica Distribution Center, Inc.
501 Prospect Street, #97
Lakewood, NJ 08701
(732) 901-3009

This Book is Dedicated To
The Memory Of
אסתר רוזה בת חי"ה ע"ה

TABLE OF CONTENTS

THE STORM

Piles of leaves swirled around gustily and settled for a moment against a garden wall. Then they were off again, dancing crazily up and down the windswept street. Trees shook and swayed alarmingly. A massive blast of wind stripped their branches bare.

Passersby held their hats firmly as they hurried by. An old lady's walking stick was torn from her hand, and she stood in one place, looking forlorn. A small boy pursued the stick and triumphantly brought it back to her. Bestowing a grateful smile on him, she let herself be blown onward.

Cra-a-a-ck! A tree had torn in two! One half came crashing downward, its splintered trunk pointing every which way. A gaping hollow appeared in the piece of trunk that was still rooted to the ground. The drama received very little attention as people raced for shelter. No one wanted to be caught outdoors when the rainstorm broke.

All at once, the heavens opened. Sheets of rain pelted down, and hit the ground like shot pellets. Umbrellas, freed of their owners, scurried past. Windshield wipers worked ineffectually to help their drivers see through the onslaught.

Tzivia Ullman pounded up the garden path, sodden and gasping. Slamming the front door behind her, she landed on the hall carpet, leaving it considerably the worse for wear. She peeled off her drenched anorak, and hung it on a hanger to dry.

"Hullooooo! Anybody home?" That was silly of her, she

thought, as soon as the words left her mouth. Of course nobody was home! How could anyone be?

She poured herself a glass of orange juice and instinctively settled in the dining room opposite Zeyde's chair. Then, mumbling a hasty *Brocha*, she drank.

This room... this chair...the whole atmosphere was full of Zeyde. You could almost feel his presence. This was where you would most often see Zeyde poring over his beloved *Seforim*. Sometimes, Tzivia would sit opposite him and watch him study. She would bring along a drink, an apple, or perhaps a biscuit. Usually, her *Brocha* came out hurriedly, in a jumble. Then Zeyde's wise eyes would twinkle at her humorously. "What train are you trying to catch? Don't rush your *Brochos* like that, he would say. "*Chazal* say that you should recite each word of a *Brocha* slowly, as if you are counting your money!"

As the rain continued to beat down outside, Tzivia cried out, "Zeyde...Why aren't you with us now, enjoying our holiday with us? I couldn't wait to spend time with you, and now you're not here!" The skies thundered and stormed and memories of yesterday came back to her with painful clarity...

****

Tzivia hammered cheerfully on the door. She rang twice for good measure. She and her parents had traveled down to London from Preston to spend a two-week winter holiday with her grandfather, Mr. Levy.

No figure appeared to peek through the opaque glass of the door. She hammered again. Her father, Rabbi Ullman, deposited the luggage on the steps.

"Shh," he whispered. "We don't want to startle Zeyde. Mummy will let us in with her key." Mrs. Ullman fished out the key from her purse, and opened the door. The Ullmans entered and looked around. All was quiet within.

"Hullooooo," called Tzivia, still in high spirits. "Zeyde, we've arrived!"

"Hush, Tzivia. Zeyde must be asleep. I'll just peep into his room." Mrs. Ullman vanished upstairs while Tzivia hauled some luggage into the up-till-then tidy hall.

Her father placed his hat onto the dining room table and glanced at an open *Sefer*, quickly proceeding to take a closer look. Tzivia knew that her father would be lost to the world for the next however long, so she went into the kitchen to put the leftover sandwiches into the fridge. Her mother clattered down the stairs.

"Zeyde's not in bed, nor is he anywhere upstairs. When I spoke to him on the telephone this morning, he told me he'd be waiting for us here." Mother and daughter regarded each other apprehensively.

"Maybe he's fallen in the garden," suggested Tzivia. A quick scramble to the windows revealed only crazy paving with no sign of human life.

Rabbi Ullman consoled them. "He can't be very far if he left this *Sefer* open. He may have merely gone shopping."

"Hmm. True. Well, I'll put the kettle on. We can have a

hot drink ready for when he comes back." Mrs. Ullman hurried out into the kitchen.

Drrrring! All three ran to welcome Mr. Levy at the front door, but they were disappointed. His Pakistani neighbor, Mrs. Tohani, stood there instead, looking somewhat downcast.

"Hello, Mrs. Rabbi," she greeted Mrs. Ullman with her usual affectionate title. "Have you heard the news?"

"No. What news?" Mrs. Ullman inquired.

"Your father's had a heart attack! He's in hospital. Mr. Drovitch was going past when he noticed your father banging on the window of the dining room. It's a good thing he has a spare key to your father's house. He let himself in and found the old man sprawled over this book on the table. Mr. Drovitch called an ambulance and had him taken in to Montgomery Hospital. Must have been a couple of hours ago."

Mrs. Ullman turned pale. She swayed on her feet. She held on to the wall to steady herself. Tzivia thrust a chair forward, and her mother sank into it gratefully. The color slowly returned to Mrs. Ullman's cheeks.

Tzivia thanked Mrs. Tohani and saw her to the door. Then she brought her mother a cup of coffee. Mrs. Ullman sipped the scalding hot coffee, watched anxiously by her husband and child.

"Are you okay now, Mummy?"

"Yes. Sorry I alarmed you; I felt a little faint. It was the shock. She broke the news so bluntly. Tutty, we'll take a mini-cab straight to Montgomery Hospital and see how my father is doing."

"Are you sure you're up to it?"

"May I come with you?" Tzivia ventured.

A silent exchange of glances took place between Tzivia's parents. Maybe this would be the last chance their daughter would have to see her grandfather... Mrs. Ullman nodded slightly and Tzivia relaxed. Picking up a *Sefer Tehillim*, she went to ring the car service.

As they drove to Montgomery Hospital, Tzivia wondered nervously if her grandfather would still be alive. Her mother was pale, but composed. Only the twisting and turning of her rings betrayed her unease. "Whatever *Hashem* does is for the best, but we have to *daven*," Mrs. Ullman stated calmly, echoing Tzivia's thoughts.

At the reception desk they asked for directions to the Intensive Care Unit. As they whooshed upstairs in the lift, Tzivia clutched her *Tehillim* tightly and murmured a fervent prayer that her grandfather would recover. Her father told them about Mr. Kitzover, a man he knew, who had had a heart attack the previous year, and was now walking around hale and hearty.

"I.C.U." were the insignificant-looking letters printed on the locked door of the ward they reached. But Tzivia knew that they indicated that her grandfather's condition was serious. Mrs. Ullman rang for attention and a uniformed nurse admitted them. "Mr. Levy's son-in-law and daughter? This way, please." She abruptly barred Tzivia's entrance. "No children are allowed in, dear. I'm sorry. There's a waiting room to the right. You're welcome to sit there until your parents are ready to go."

The waiting room consisted of monotonous gray seats and mint-green walls adorned with several cheerful posters. Tzivia gave free vent to her tears as she recited *Tehillim*. The words blurred on the page.

After some time, her father emerged, silent and pale. He and Tzivia left the hospital and took a bus home. Mrs. Ullman wanted to stay a bit longer with her father. Upon arriving at Mr. Levy's home, Rabbi Ullman immediately began phoning *Eretz Yisroel* to ask for the blessings of various *Tzadikim* for his father-in-law's recovery. Tzivia flopped onto the floor of the living room, totally drained.

The ringing doorbell shook her out of her reverie. With dragging steps, she went to unlock the door. A tall girl stood in the entranceway, smiling widely at her. Her short, fair hair was drawn back with a hair-band. "*Sholom Aleichem*, Tzivia," she said.

"Zisy Drovitch! How good to see you again! Especially at such a time!" Tzivia gulped down the lump that threatened to rise again in her throat. She really was happy to see her old friend, who lived across the street from Zeyde.

"I know, Tzivia; your grandfather's illness must be very difficult to bear. But we'll talk soon... First, I have to deliver what my mother sent."

It was only now that Tzivia noticed that her friend was holding a covered tray. Zisy placed her treasures on the kitchen worktop, and uncovered them. "This is vegetable soup; that's grilled fish. Here's rice, salad, and some fruit cocktail. Enjoy!"

Inhaling the delicious aromas, Tzivia realized that she was ravenously hungry. "It's so sweet of your mother to think of us. Thanks a million!"

****

Mrs. Ullman arrived home in the evening, exhausted. The meal provided by their thoughtful next-door neighbors revived her, and she talked to her daughter over a cup of tea. "Zeyde's condition is stable, which means there's no change. We'll probably stick to the following schedule: I will spend most of the day with him in hospital, and Tutty will take over in the evenings. I'm sorry; you will be on your own for much of the next few days."

"Don't worry about me, Mummy. I'll manage just fine. I'll visit Zisy next door if I'm lonely. Besides which, I'd love to leaf through some of Zeyde's old papers. He has an old chest in the loft that I've been meaning to explore, what do you say to that?" Tzivia tried to act as though she was just fine. Her mother had enough to worry about without Tzivia adding to her load. However, there was no reply. Her mother was nodding drowsily.

They soon retired for the night. Tzivia tossed and turned, unable to relax. As the first rays of daylight broke the horizon, she finally fell asleep.

To judge by her mother's haggard face the next morning, she, too, had not slept much. She had no news for her daughter. "I've just rung the hospital. There's no change. *Boruch Hashem* for small mercies - at least it's not any worse. Well," she said, rising from a kitchen chair, "I'm off to the hospital now. Tutty will be back soon." Mrs. Ullman waved goodbye.

Tzivia was momentarily at a loss. What would she do with herself on her own? Ah, yes, the chest in the loft. She would take it down right now. She did not expect any exciting discoveries, but still, she thought she might find something interesting; a few old photographs, perhaps?

How was Tzivia to know that the contents of the chest would change the lives of several people forever...?

MRS VIRTSCHAFT GIVES ADVICE

Tzivia swung the beam of the flashlight around the dark loft. Cobwebs hung from the sloping ceiling. Daylight filtered in from a small gap in the roof, where a tile had fallen off in the storm. It added very little light to the room, but her yellow torchlight caused thousands of particles of dust to dance crazily in its arching, moving beam. Beyond the cobwebs stood a dusty, grey chest, its grimy domed lid festooned with rust. Then the light flitted over a dusty chest. Tzivia swept the torch over the tiled ceiling, hesitated a moment, and returned the light to the chest. It seemed to beckon to her – did it contain a treasure? It was time to explore its contents.

A six-legged creature scurried away from her hand as she reached for the chest. Tzivia stifled a shriek, but she tightly clutched the box with one arm and carefully descended the ladder. What secrets did the treasure-box contain, she wondered curiously as she pried open the curved lid with a screwdriver. She had long wanted to discover what was inside of this old chest that sat in the loft. One more push with the screwdriver and the lid suddenly gave with a creak, revealing— not the crown jewels—but a sheaf of faded papers. "Is that all?" she grimaced, disappointed.

Rummaging through the yellowed papers, Tzivia glanced at the almost illegible print. The letters were written in ink, and parts of the top page were indecipherable. The moisture in the damp loft had probably smudged the words. She fetched Zeyde's reading-glasses to use as a type of magnifying glass, and began to read:

9

Dear Mummy and little Perele (That's Mummy's name! Tzivia realized with a start. This letter must have been written a long time ago if it calls Mummy 'little!')

I am far from you but close in spirit. Boruch Hashem, *my mission was mostly successful. Apologies for not having written to you ——— but it was essential that no one know of my whereabouts, for the safety of all concerned. I know it is hard for you——-but I will write a detailed account of my adventure.*

——-vanished————-   ——————-(illegible) I traveled to an orphanage known as "Refuge for the Homeless." Our group of ——————- had heard terrible cases of several Jewish children disappearing off the streets of Yemen. They were never heard of again. In fact, one unfortunate family had traced their child to this orphanage. However, the priests then told the police that they have diplomatic immunity. "You have no right to enter or search our building," the priests insisted. The police were powerless to act!

We received reliable information that one of the priests at the orphanage would chat with children on the streets, striking up a friendship with them. In a matter of weeks, —— ——— days, the child would vanish.

I was approached in the strictest secrecy by M————-, with the suggestion that I find a job at the orphanage. I was to do all in my power to assist these unfortunate children to escape and to return them to their grieving families.

Tzivia flipped to the next page. Here, she saw, the

writing was completely legible. She sat down and returned to the letter.

On May ninth, I arrived at the orphanage and presented myself to the Father of the Order, wearing local Arab dress. The black-garbed priest scrutinised me suspiciously. He spoke in an oily, over-friendly manner. "How can I help you, my son?" I said that I was looking for work. He took in every detail of my appearance. I assumed a dumb look. "I'm good at peeling potatoes and carrots," I said. "And if your cook is ill, I can even help with the cooking."

He almost smiled! Then he said that perhaps I could help serve the meals too. They were short-staffed at the moment. This was more than I had dared hope for. I would have an opportunity to meet the children personally. A smile must have appeared on my lips for the Father snapped at me, "You won't be paid very much here. We can't afford a lot."

"That's okay," I said, shrugging my shoulders nonchalantly, disguising my eagerness. "A bed and a meal once a day, plus just a bit of spending money is all I need." He agreed and called someone named Thomas to show me to my working quarters. He rang a little brass bell on his desk.

Thomas is a mean-looking fellow, with a face like a bulldog. He ordered me to follow him.

Tzivia stopped reading, and gasped. The chest had contained a treasure after all! She had to show this letter to someone – she would run over to Zisy and share her find. They would read it together.

Latching Zeyde's garden gate closed, she turned—and stopped, startled. A broad-shouldered elderly man in a striped black and white coat and woolen gray hat was squatting on the ground outside No. 45. His beard was unkempt, and his eyes stared sightlessly from under shaggy gray eyebrows.

Tzivia was taken aback! Zeyde had Arab neighbors! What a surprise that was! She rang long and hard at Zisy's door.

Zisy appeared, with the baby on her hip, looking flustered. "Take him, quickly!" She thrust the baby into Tzivia's arms and vanished. Tzivia stood there, astonished. Only then did she become aware of the terrifying screams coming from somewhere in the house.

"What's going on?" she called fearfully. "Zisy! Zisy! Are you okay? Where are you? Zisy, answer me! Are you okay?" Was there a burglar in the place? Had someone swallowed poison? Her mind in a whirl, she walked toward the screams with the baby in her arms.

The shouting was coming from the kitchen. Zisy was splashing her little brother Gavrielli with water in the kitchen sink. He was gulping at the water, screeching and struggling to get out of the sink and out of Zisy's hold. Tzivia nearly dropped the baby, who tugged cheerfully at her hair. "Wh-what... is going on?" she stammered.

"CALL HATZOLAH!" Zisy shouted, continuing to splash cupfuls of running tap water onto her hapless brother. Gavrielli screamed, "No! No!" and kicked at his sister.

"Have you gone mad?" Tzivia approached her friend, horrified by this scene of torture.

"Just do as I say!" her friend said, urgently, rivulets of water dripping down her dress. "Tell them Gavrielli's spilled a boiling-hot plate of soup over himself!"

Tzivia dialed Hatzolah's number with trembling fingers, hooking the baby-walker forward with her leg and depositing the happy, oblivious baby into it. Trying to ignore the background howling, she blurted out the details to the man on the other end.

The howls of the panic-stricken child in the sink increased together with the amount of water in the rapidly filling sink. "Fill up the baby bath with cold water. Quickly!" Zisy hissed.

Unearthly shrieks punctuated by gulping accompanied Tzivia's rush to the bathroom. Fumbling the white plastic baby bath into the big bath, she turned the cold water full on. "Zisy, the bath is almost full! Put him in already!" she called, hoping that Zisy could hear her.

Her friend ran into the bathroom, clutching her little brother, whose screams had subsided into sobs at the brief respite from the terrible nightmare. Then Zisy dumped the little boy unceremoniously into the freezing baby-bath, clothes and all. The screams started again with redoubled force.

"Ah! At last! Hatzolah's here!" Tzivia breathed a heartfelt sigh of relief at the chime of the doorbell. She sprinted to the door and threw it open. She was almost knocked flat by the enormous woman who swept in. "Gut morrrning! I come to borrow a pecket of - Hey! Vot's dat screaming??" The woman's eyes bulged at the unearthly wail.

"It's all right, Mrs. Virtschaft. Everything's okay." Tzivia groaned inwardly. Of all times, this well-meaning neighbor had to arrive *now,* in the middle of everything! "Gavrielli's just burnt himself. Hatzolah will be here any minute now."

"*Oy vay! Oy vay*! Vot a terrible 'ting to heppen! Vere is de poor *bubbele*? Take me to de little *sheyfele*!" she boomed, wringing her hands together.

"Don't worry, Mrs. Virtschaft. He's in the bath." Tzivia tried in vain to calm the woman. A piercing screech directed the portly neighbor to the bathroom.

"Vot? You left him in der *bood* by himself? Vot a *meshugene* 'ting to do! He could... *Chas Vesholom*... I don't vant to say de vords! I can't *farshtei* you youngsters! Never leave a baby alone in *dem bood*!" She lumbered into the bathroom as rapidly as her ample girth would allow.

Tzivia bit down an angry retort. Zisy had stayed with her brother. And even if she had left him alone in the bath, someone would have had to open the door for Hatzolah!

"*Oy vay! Mein hartz*!" the fat woman slapped her hand on her chest as if she was saying "*Al cheyt*." "Vot do mein eyes see? A *kleine yingel* in *dem bood* mit all his *clozes*! *Meshugeh*! Tek him out stretavay! Vot a *meshugaas*!" She stretched out her bejeweled hands to the frightened little boy. "Come to me, Gavrielli! Come to Aunty Lali! Aunty Lali vill tek you out from dis horrible *bood*!"

Gavrielli took one look at the hugely obese woman and burst into a fresh torrent of tears. Tzivia looked on helplessly as the woman started hoisting the terrified child out of the baby bath despite Zisy's protests.

"No! No! The best treatment for burns is to sit the person in a cold bath and splash them with cold water on the burn. Please, let him be!" Zisy pulled her shivering brother back into the baby bath. The exhausted child wept anew.

"I never heard such a *meshugaas* in my *gantze leben*!" the woman's triple chins wobbled in outrage. "Come to me, *yingele*!" she stretched out her plump hands again and pulled the boy out.

"Just a minute, please," a man said authoritatively from behind them. Everybody turned round. A bearded man was placing a Hatzolah box on the tiled floor. "I saw the door open and took the liberty of coming in unannounced. Would you like to put the child back into the bath? I'll have a look at him."

Mrs. Virtschaft gasped audibly and dropped the child back in with a splash that soaked her. Zisy sighed in relief. Tzivia realized that her friend had begun to tremble from the shock of all that had happened. She put her arm round her friend's shoulders.

The Hatzolah man examined the boy. "There's hardly a blister or a blotch on his chest or leg!" he exclaimed. "You acted very sensibly by putting him in a cold bath. The best thing one can do for a burn is to soak the affected area in cold water for fifteen minutes to an hour."

Zisy flushed uncomfortably as Mrs. Virtschaft slapped her on the back. "Oy vay, *mein kind*! Do you forgive me? Good girl. Oy vay. I don't feel good. It's *mein hartz*."

The Hatzolah man, gently replacing Gavrielli into the baby bath, looked up, concerned. Was he about to be provided with another patient? But the enormous woman shook her head, her chins shaking in unison. "I'm okay. Bye bye, Gavrielli and everyvun." With an ungainly tread, she departed, and attention returned to the little boy, who was now hiccupping quietly.

"Keep him in the bath as long as you can, even up to an hour, adding cold water occasionally. The swelling should go down. If the child complains of pain later on, take him to your doctor. Are you all right now, young man?"

"OY VAY! OY VAY!" A panic-stricken shout made the two girls jump.

The Hatzolah man leapt to his feet. He was out in the hall in seconds. Was the old woman having a heart attack?

"Oy vay! Oy vay!" The two girls at his heels were shaken at the sight of Mrs. Virtschaft bent nearly double. Their gaze dropped to the floor - there was the baby shredding a box of white tissues and stuffing them into his mouth. "De baby vas eating a hanky! Oy vay! Oy vay! You're a Hatzolah man - do someting! A *halbe* hanky is in dem baby's tummy!"

Tzivia and Zisy took one look at each other and burst into fits of laughter. Their peals of merriment set Gavrielli off in the bathroom, though he had no idea why they were guffawing. Even the Hatzolah man smiled.

Mrs. Virtschaft's chins wobbled in indignation. "Has everyvun gone *meshuga*? He's svallowed a *halbe* hanky and you are leffing?"

Zisy choked on a giggle and cried, "Mrs. Virtschaft, please don't get insulted. We're not laughing at you; *Chas Vesholom*! The baby is always eating hankies. Whenever there's a tissue on the floor, he eats it before anyone has noticed. The doctor says he won't come to any harm." The Hatzolah man had, meanwhile, hooked his finger into the baby's mouth and pulled out a small but sopping white mass.

Shrugging her massive shoulders, Mrs. Virtschaft departed, muttering, "Ah *meshugene velt* ve live in!" The Hatzolah man left, as well, after repeating his instructions.

Soon after, Tzivia heard a key in the lock and went into the hallway to see who was letting themselves into the house.

Mrs. Drovitch greeted her with a warm smile. "Hallo, Tzivia, how's your grandfather?" she inquired, putting down her shopping bags.

"Still the same. No change, as far as I know."

Mrs. Drovitch put a motherly arm around her shoulders. "We're all *davening* for him. And Tzivia, feel free to join us for all our meals and whenever you feel like company."

"Mummy! Oh, Mummy! Is that you? I must tell you what

happened!" Zisy called from the bathroom.

Tzivia slipped out of the house, realizing that she was no longer needed. "Tzivia!" she heard her name being called as she crossed the street. Zisy was waving a sheaf of papers at her. "These are yours."

"Oh yes! I forgot! I came to show you this fascinating letter I found in my Zeyde's chest in his loft. You probably won't have time to join me in reading it now, will you?"

"Hold on a sec." Soon, having obtained permission from her mother, Zisy joined her friend. The two sat down on the front stoop of Mr. Levy's quiet house for an enthralling read.

FLIGHT!

Thomas led the way down staircases that seemed to lead into the bowels of the earth. The pungent odor of non-kosher meat hit me as soon as we entered the kitchen. A mountain of a man stood over the stove, ladle in hand. He was stirring the mixture with vigorous strokes. "Umm, delicious!" he slurped a spoonful of the steamy broth. "Here, taste some!" he thrust the spoon at me.

"Er, no. Sorry. I'm a vegetarian." I groped for an excuse.

"Then Thomas. You must try some of this," the mountainous cook waved his ladle at Thomas. The bulldog merely screwed up his face in distaste and shook his head disdainfully. "Not for me. This is your new kitchen-worker, Abdul." With a haughty glance in my direction, he exited, slamming the door.

"Unpleasant fellow, that!" the cook shook my hand, leaving it squashed almost to a pulp. "Pleased to have you with us. You say your name is Abdul? Abdul, would you mind peeling that sack of potatoes in the corner?" he said. He whipped out a peeler from a grimy drawer, and I set to work.

I had never peeled so many potatoes in my life, Mummy, not even for Pesach. My hands were sore by the time I thankfully reached the last layer of potatoes in the sack.

"We've close to eighty orphans," explained the cook, transferring the peeled potatoes into a pot of boiling water

with a splash.

"All religions?" I asked casually, nursing a bleeding finger, which I had peeled in error.

He said, "Oh yes. We have all sorts, Moslems, Christians, and Jews. They come to us from all over." Dipping his fingers into a salad, he cocked his head to one side and stared off into space. "Needs more salt," he commented and sprinkled some into the salad. He sampled the salad once again with his unwashed fingers and nodded, wiping his hands on his greasy, faded, once-white apron. I wondered how he could "taste" food with his fingers!

The dinner-gong rang a while later. Thomas wheeled in a metal trolley and I helped the cook load the huge pots of food onto it. "You're to serve with me," Thomas tossed the words at me over his shoulder and jerked his thumb toward the door.

Together, we pushed the trolley up several ramps until we reached the dining room. The sounds of childish chatter surrounded us. I looked around with interest. Children of all shapes and sizes were seated at round tables. They were eagerly awaiting their food. I felt many pairs of eyes on me as I wheeled the trolley to the wall, accompanied by Thomas. I waited. He folded his arms and leaned indifferently against the wall.

I soon found out why we were waiting. The entire room hushed as the Father made a dramatic entrance. He was followed by a group of solemn monks. Taking his place on the dais, he bade the assemblage to "arise for Grace before meals." Everyone rose simultaneously to their feet, clasped their hands and prayed with bowed heads.

20

The children proceeded to line up at the trolley, holding out their plates. How on earth was I going to locate a single Jewish child among all these children? Scanning the crowd, I whispered a brief prayer. Then I had a brainstorm.

"Would you like some meat?" I asked each little boy in the queue.

"No thanks," one replied.

"Why not?" I said.

"Don't like meat," he said, his little nose crinkling.

"Would you like some meat?" I asked the next one.

"Yes, please," he replied.

"And you?" I went from one orphan to the next. They all said yes.

Then one orphan, with a large forehead and soulful brown eyes, answered my query with "Oh no. I can't have meat!"

"Why not?" I quickly inquired, with a quickening of interest.

"I... I just can't, that's all," he said.

"But are you ill? Not allowed to eat meat under doctor's orders?" I pushed him.

The boy gazed into my eyes as if unsure of whether or not he could trust me. With a wary glance at Thomas, he whispered, "I'm Jewish. It's not kosher."

A surge of joy swept through me. The experiment had worked! Thomas glared at me, menacingly. "You're holding up the queue! Quit the talking!"

The little boy moved hastily off, but not before I had studied his face well and resolved to speak to him again at the earliest opportunity. A monk sternly rebuked me. "I am Brother Paul. I am in charge of mealtime. You are not allowed to talk to the boys. It slows down the meal for the entire orphanage."

"My apologies," I said blandly, and continued serving. The children ate in silence. Compote was served for dessert, and then, after the hall had emptied, Thomas and I piled the dirty crockery onto the trolley.

As I wheeled the trolley back to the kitchen, my mind buzzed with all sorts of possibilities. I would reveal myself to the boy and enlist his aid in discovering the identities of all the other Jewish children here. I had already concocted a vague plan to help them escape, but my ideas needed work. How could I speak to the boy again even while avoiding the scrutiny of the many monks and orphans? Why, I didn't even know the little boy's name, yet! I decided to keep watch near the bedrooms. If I were asked to explain my presence, I would claim to have lost my way to my own room (which I shared with the cook).

While some of the boys were preparing for bed, I stood unobtrusively at the end of the darkened corridor and looked out for "my" boy. I waited and waited but he was not among the many that passed. Perhaps he went to bed at a later time, I mused, watching the boys scurry about in their pajamas.

Then I dared not tarry any longer— for there was Brother Paul heading purposefully toward me. I rushed down the corridor, sped down the staircase and ducked into the first doorway I could see. I found myself in a huge library. Crowded bookshelves reached to the ceiling. Almost all the lights were extinguished. I noticed, suddenly, a boy bent over his work. He lifted his head. Brown, soulful eyes locked with mine.

"It's you!" I exclaimed in delight. "I've been trying to find you all evening!"

The boy whispered, "I've been punished. The Father noticed that I wasn't saying Grace Before Meals. I think they keep a special eye on me because I'm Jewish. They've put me into solitary confinement for two hours with an essay to do."

"Why didn't you say Grace?" I took his chin in my cupped hands and looked deeply into his eyes.

"Because I'm Jewish and I can't pray to false gods," he stated proudly, defiance sparking his eyes.

"Aren't you afraid I'm going to repeat this conversation to the monks?" I said.

"No. I trust you," the little boy looked at me searchingly.

"I have a feeling that you're a good person."

"To tell you the truth, I'm Jewish too," I said in a very low voice.

"You are?" his mouth fell open.

"Yes," I told him. "My name is... Well, I'd better not tell you my name, just in case you're questioned about me. I'm here to help you, and any other Jewish children being held here, escape to a free country where you'll be able to start a new life with Orthodox Jewish people."

The boy went limp. He let me hold him as he gave vent on my shoulder to his long pent-up emotions. My shirt was soon soaked with his tears. Then he spoke. "I've been here for six months already. They cut off my Payos, took away my cap and Tzitzis," he sobbed. "They try to make me work on Shabbos and eat non-kosher food. But I haven't given in! I try to keep the Mitzvos together with my friends Daoud (David) and Sulimein (Saadya). I am Yosef Al-Tiri. Here they call me Mohammed."

I told him, "I'm thrilled to meet you and I want you to introduce me to the other two Jewish boys as soon as possible. I have an escape route mapped out in my head, but I need to know one urgent thing – Is there a time when the supervision here is more lax than usual?"

The boy pondered, placing his pencil on his essay, which was written in a bold, yet spidery handwriting. Then he said, "This Tuesday, we'll be having our annual fancy-dress party. All the children will be there, including most of the staff. Yes, that would seem the best time to escape. Oh, I'd better finish my essay; Brother John will soon be along to let me out of here."

"We meet here tomorrow, then?" I asked. He nodded. "At the same time, with your friends."

He frowned. "I don't know. It's not easy to get them here at this time of night. What if we come to the kitchen with some excuse? Tomorrow, perhaps, during the time when we do the gardening?" I agreed.

With a hasty "good night" and "may Hashem be with you," I left the library and returned to the kitchen.

"Where have YOU been?" a scowling Thomas greeted me. "We need help with washing-up! Lazy lout!" he railed against me, as I rolled up my sleeves and went over to a sink full of plates and soapy suds.

The good-humored cook chuckled, his double chins wobbling in mirth. "Leave him alone, Thomas! You need to put on more weight, like me; you'll be a lot more cheerful. Take life easy; let others breathe!" Let me tell you, Mummy, I am grateful for the cook and his happy attitude. Thomas is frightening and the boys shrink in fear of him.

****

The next morning, I was scraping fish-scales from raw, slippery fish, when three young boys, one of whom was Yosef, tapped respectfully at the kitchen door.

"Excuse me," said Yosef with a wink in my direction,

"would you have some carrot-tops or old potatoes that we could plant in the garden?"

The cook deposited a bag of flour into an enormous waist-to-floor sized machine and nodded at the boys. "Abdul," he pointed toward the larder. "Give the boys some old vegetables from the larder."

"Thank you, Cook," the boys chorused. Washing my hands, I gladly led them into the chilly larder, where the metal-latticed window gave off a cool breeze.

"This is Daoud and Sulimein," Yosef introduced his friends. Daoud was tall and gangly. He was eleven and had been in the orphanage since the age of seven. Sulimein, a short, tubby boy, eight years old, smiled politely at me.

"Precious Jewish children," I whispered. "Would you like to leave this place and start a new life in a Torah community?"

"Sure!" and "Of course!" "When and where?" The eager words burst forth from the boys simultaneously.

"Soon, with Hashem's help. Here are some carrots and potatoes." I handed each boy several vegetables. "I'll let Yosef, er, Mohammed, know of any developments. It is possible that we'll make our escape on the day of the fancy-dress party," I said.

Their faces glowing, the boys thanked me and departed.

"Who's on gate-duty every night?" I asked the cook innocently, while I dried the piles of dishes, moments later. I hoped that he would not become suspicious.

"Thomas in the evenings and Al-Hussein during the day. Why?" the cook inquired, licking out the last drops of some meat mixture.

"Did I hear my name mentioned?" Thomas barked, gruffly, striding into the kitchen.

"Yes, you did." I replied confidently. "I was only thinking that you would probably prefer watching the fancy-dress party instead of being on gate-duty."

"You bet I would. They always leave me the dirty work in this place!" he growled.

"Would you like me to take your place?" I asked, trying to sound guiltless.

"Mmmm. I wouldn't mind. Thanks." His bulldog-like face creased into what was meant to be a smile. It was only a slight improvement over his scowl. "I start at seven p.m. and go on till one a.m. Then we close up for the night."

"No problem," I said as I rubbed a plate vigorously, attempting to mask my glee. It was all going so easily, without a hitch. All I needed to do now was to hire a horse and covered wagon to transport my forbidden cargo to the station. We would take the late train and then ... goodbye to the orphanage. Could anything go wrong now?

****

A thick snow was falling on Tuesday morning when I awoke. I nervously checked my plans again. At seven o'clock this evening, when the orphans would be milling about in the great hall trying to guess who was who ... we would make our escape. My three Jewish boys would meet at the little cubicle at the gate, where I would be on guard-duty. The horse and wagon I had hired would be awaiting us, not far from the orphanage. We would take the seven-thirty train. It was a fast train, and we would, with Hashem's help, be able to elude any pursuit once the train set off. If all went well, we would be in Europe within a few days.

A feeling of foreboding swept over me, but I could not explain why. Something was bothering me, but what? The plans seemed to be running smoothly. Nothing could go wrong now, or so I hoped. Only time would tell.

The hours ticked past very slowly. Dinnertime came and went, along with the normal chores of peeling, washing up, and cleaning the dining room. The monks took charge of setting up the decorations for the party that evening. Time seemed to drag on slower than ever before.

It was ten to seven. I headed toward the gate and exchanged places with Al-Hussein, who wished me a cheery good night and disappeared into the darkness.

So far, so good.

I sat on my perch and uttered all the chapters of Tehillim *that I knew by heart. We had to succeed. "This might be the only chance these boys will ever have of returning to*

Yiddishkeit. *Please help them to escape,"* I davened, *drumming my fingers nervously on the little desk beside the window.*

Five to seven. Nobody had yet approached the gate, not to go in, nor to leave. I hoped that the staff would be so busy with the party that they would not realize the absence of a guard at the gate, once I had left with the boys. Snowflakes whirled crazily about, alighting velvet-like on the window.

It was one minute to seven. A head suddenly appeared at my window wearing a clown mask. I slid open the window and peered out. The mask was raised and Daoud whispered, "It's me, Daoud." I silently let him into my cubicle and he crouched down on the floor so as not to be seen from outside.

The minutes ticked past as my patience drained away. It was four minutes past seven. "Where are they?" I whispered. "We're meant to be in the wagon by now! We'll miss the train at this rate!" I felt more impatient than I ever had in my entire life.

Ten past seven! What had happened to them? I feared that something terrible had indeed occurred to upset my plans. Should I leave with Daoud alone? But what would happen to the other two boys? No, I must strengthen my Bitachon *and wait, I thought.*

An urgent tap on the window, which was now blocked by the heavy snow, made me jump. It was them! "At last, Sulimein! I was beginning to give up on you! Where were you? And where is Yosef?" I asked.

The boy stamped the snow off his shoes and sat heavily in my chair. "Yosef is missing! We must leave without him!"

"Missing? What do you mean 'missing'?" I exploded, slamming my fist into my hand.

I was shocked by his answer. He said, "I looked all over for him, but I couldn't find him anywhere. Thomas, that evil fellow, asked me what I was doing in our room, instead of being in the hall with everyone. 'I've come for my friend, Mohammed,' I explained. 'I want to masquerade with him.'

"'The Jew boy is gone!' Thomas jeered. 'I drove him to the station today together with two monks. A family in Greece is adopting him. You won't be seeing him again.' Abdul, I think he was telling the truth."

I was incredulous. Our only chance of helping Yosef escape had disappeared together with him. I mourned the loss of a precious Jewish child to Yiddishkeit.

But it was getting late. These two boys must still be brought to freedom. Overcoming my sadness, I opened the door of the cubicle to allow us all to leave the orphanage forever. I quickly drew back. Someone was approaching through the swirling snowflakes! "Get down on the floor!" I hissed at the two boys. I promptly covered them with my coat.

The cook lumbered up to us. I stepped hastily out of the cubicle and stood blocking the doorway. "Hullo," I greeted him nonchalantly. "What brings you here in such pleasant weather?" I hoped desperately that he would not notice that I was coatless.

"Salaam Aleikum, *my friend.*" He said, and he handed me a covered tray, which was quickly mantled with snow-crystals. "I thought of you, all alone at your post at the gate and I felt sorry for you. You're missing all the festivities. So I thought, what can I bring you that you'll enjoy? Here's a sampling of all the goodies at the party."

"That is really nice of you!" I clapped the cook on the back, yearning for him to leave.

"Go on, uncover the tray and take a look at the delicacies. Shall we have a look together in your cubicle, out of the snow?" he said with a broad smile.

Pasting a grin to my bloodless lips, I smiled and said in an undertone, "I hardly think the two of us would fit in there together!" How could I be rid of him?

He chuckled and deposited the tray into my hands. He said, "Here. Sit down in your hut and enjoy this mouthwatering food."

I made a show of licking my lips. "Thanks a million. It's nice to have a good friend in the place."

The cook chuckled, his belly wobbling. He said, "Have to get some meat on you - you're such a skinny bones. Well, 'bye." Then he waddled off into the blizzard. After several moments had passed, I opened the door to the cubicle and signed to the boys to follow me.

I unlocked the high orphanage gate and swung it closed

behind us, making sure to leave the key in the lock so that they would be delayed if they tried to pursue us.

The wagon driver was awaiting us close by, his horse trying to shake off the swirling snowflakes. The man nodded at us to board the wagon, raising his eyebrows somewhat at the two boys in fancy dress. I provided no explanation. We trotted along as the children stripped off their costumes and masks, revealing their usual apparel underneath.

"Can't you go a little faster?" I called out to the wagon driver.

"In this weather, my friend, no vehicle can go any faster, except maybe the train," he said. His whip lashed out, however, and his meager horse increased its pace.

We were traveling slowly, as the snow fell ever more thickly. We gladly sheltered under the canopy of the wagon. The temperature was freezing, and we huddled together for warmth.

My heart felt icy cold in company with the weather. What a tragedy that Yosef, that sweet, endearing child, was to be adopted by a gentile family. How would he ever return to Yiddishkeit? "The ways of Hashem are hidden," I murmured. The boys drew closer together and looked fearfully at the blinding snowstorm raging about us.

Would we be stopped before we could enter the train? Had the police been alerted about the disappearance of two orphans and a newly employed worker?

We had reached the road leading up to the station, but we could not ascend the hill. At the flick of the driver's whip, the mare strained to pull us uphill, but each time the wagon slid gently backward on the icy road. The driver jumped down, skidded on an icy patch and landed on his face. With remarkable agility, he picked himself up and guided the horse patiently up the slope. About halfway up the road, the nag refused to go any further. It was just too difficult.

"This is as far as I can take you," the driver patted his nag's head as he spoke. "She needs to get home to her stable and some straw now." I paid him and quickly hid the discarded costumes under a snow-covered bush.

I linked arms with the two boys, and we climbed the hill and entered the station.

Only one ticket clerk sat behind the glass partition attending to the long queue. I deposited the boys on a bench near the doors (so they could flee if need be) and joined the queue.

"Seven-thirty p.m," screamed the large station clock. We would miss the train! But then I overheard someone say that the train had not yet arrived. What a relief! Boruch Hashem!

I waited in an agony of impatience as the noisy queue inched forward. You might have thought that few people would travel in such weather, but it appeared as if the whole world had decided to travel by rail that evening. "Impossible to get anywhere tonight other than by rail," the clerk was explaining to a woman two places ahead of me. "The train will be delayed by another half an hour, however, as snow must be cleared from the tracks, but otherwise it's business as usual."

Another half an hour! My stomach lurched at the thought. A lot could happen in half an hour, including my arrest and the return of the boys, under heavy guard, to the orphanage. But what could we do? We were totally dependent on the mercy of the Ribono Shel Olam. *I purchased an adult ticket and two child fares.*

We settled down to wait in the enclosed waiting room, along with many others. Was that old man in the corner watching us or was he actually dozing? The others were too busy talking or sleeping to take much notice of us. I kept watching the door anxiously - would the police get here before we left?

At last! A collective sigh of relief sounded as the train chugged into the station. Hordes of people scrambled on to the train, lugging bags and parcels. We were traveling light, carrying nothing but a sack full of food and drink that I had taken from the orphanage kitchen.

At eight-oh-five pm, the whistle finally blew. We could not stop peering from the windows in search of any pursuers coming through the blizzard. Boruch Hashem, *there were none. As the train chugged out of the station, I hugged the two boys and whispered a grateful thank you to* Hakodosh Boruch Hu. *At the same time, I grieved for the one child whom we had left behind, and offered a silent* Tefilla *that some day, some time, in the near future, Yosef, too, would return to* Yiddishkeit.

My dear family, I will be home in several weeks, Im Yirtze Hashem. *We are laying low until the hunt for the two boys is off. Perele, I know that you will be a good girl and help your Mummy.*

From your husband and Daddy, who misses you very much.

THE PHOTOGRAPH

"What a discovery!" Zisy was awed. "This letter must have been laying in your Zeyde's attic for years without anyone knowing about it!"

Tzivia rose from her grandfather's front step as she carefully placed the letter into an envelope. "I never knew that my grandfather was involved in helping rescue Jewish children!"

A neighbor passed by bearing a cake. "Oh no! I forgot; the cleaner's coming!" the woman clapped a hand to her mouth.

"Good morning, Mrs. Zahava," Zisy greeted her respectfully.

"Hello, Zisy. Zisy," the woman hesitated. "Could I ask you a favor? I was about to bring a cake to the Teimani couple living at No.45, but I forgot something important at home. Would you kindly take in the cake for me?"

"Of course," Zisy took the cake carefully. "I'll see that it gets there."

The two approached the Arab-looking man in his striped coat and woolen hat, sitting on a cushion in his front garden. He raised his head and stared sightlessly in their direction. "So! The man was Teimani, not Arab! I was scared for nothing," thought Tzivia.

"May we speak to your wife?" Tzivia inquired, her heart in her mouth.

He nodded and called something. A lady in black, flowing robes, her hair totally concealed by a gaily-colored scarf, welcomed them. She had an old-young face—a face lined with wrinkles revealing much pain and sadness, yet a glimpse of a youthful smile showed through. "*Salaam Aleikum.*"

"Hello, I'm Tzivia Ullman and this is my friend Zisy Drovitch. We have brought you a cake from Mrs. Zahava."

"*Todah Rabah*! Please come in," the Teimani woman showed them into the small, cozy flat. There she proudly pointed to the photographs on the mantelpiece. "This my husband. This me. My Chinah - Teimani wedding." In the photograph, she wore a black hooded robe with gold tassels, and stood beside an older woman bearing a plant-pot with a lighted candle inside "for *Mazal*," she explained.

Pride of place was a photo in a plain, plastic frame. The Teimani woman looked from it to the girls and was silent. It was a photo of a little boy, approximately six years old. "He's adorable. Is that your son?" Zisy asked, curiously.

The Teimani woman grimaced with pain. She said nothing. Zisy realized that she had said something wrong and quickly changed the subject. "How long will you be here in England?"

"Till doctor help my husband. One month, maybe more. People kind to us. Give us chairs, table. We want to go back to *Eretz Yisroel* after. *Shalom, Giveret,*" she looked up as Mrs.

Zahava entered, bearing a bag of groceries. *"Todah Rabah."* The Teimani woman took out some money and paid for the groceries. Mrs. Zahava grinned cheerfully at the girls.

"Hallo, girls. Thanks for bringing in the cake for me," she said as she accepted the money and walked with them to the door.

"Todah Rabah, come again." The elderly woman led them past her blind husband, who was murmuring something quietly. Tzivia caught the sounds of several words of *Tehillim.*

Blindness ... She blinked in the cold winter sunlight. The watery blue sky was adorned with a V-formation of squawking geese flying overhead. The bare bushes lining the gardens nodded in the breeze. Pigeons pecked the earth in search of food. The refreshing green of the evergreen trees was a soothing balm to her heart. The world had never seemed quite so fresh and appealing. She was suddenly so grateful for the gift of sight.

Mrs. Zahava nodded at them. "It's nice of you two to have taken the cake to Mrs. Al-Tiri. I'm sure she appreciates it."

Tzivia stared. "Did you say ... Mrs. Al-Tiri?? But... that's the name of the little boy, Yosef, in my grandfather's letter! Could it be his family?"

Zisy was equally shocked. "Mrs. Zahava, did you see that photo in there of a little boy? Do you know any details about him?"

"It's a sad tale. The little boy in the photograph was their only son. He was snatched away from them. He was only seven."

Zisy's eyes opened wide. "How did it happen?"

"He was on his way to a friend, but he never arrived. The parents were out of their minds with worry. The police searched high and low, but he had vanished without a trace. 'Yosef! Yosef!' his parents screamed. Their friends fanned out in many directions and searched too, but to no avail.

"A couple of neighbors reported having seen a European car on a nearby road, which was unusual in Yemen, but there were no other clues. The boy was gone. His parents were wild with grief. They could not stop crying. Their only child - kidnapped!"

Tzivia felt a lump rise in her throat. "How tragic."

"Yes. A lead came six months later. A gentile tourist reported having visited an orphanage near Yemen. A Jewish child had grabbed the tourist by the arm and exclaimed, 'I am Yosef! Take me home to my Daddy and Mummy in Yemen!' When the tourist asked the priest in charge of the orphanage for an explanation, he was told, 'The child's parents died in a crash.'

"On the tourist's next visit to the orphanage, Yosef was no longer there. They told him that the child had been transferred to a sister orphanage overseas. The tourist contacted the Jewish community in Yemen and gave over the details. The police were contacted. They arrived at the orphanage with a search warrant, but were told by the priests, who were missionaries, 'We have diplomatic immunity as we are foreigners to this country. You have no right to search our orphanage.' The police left it at that. They were not interested in causing an international scandal. Why should it bother them that a Jewish child was missing in Yemen? There were other occasional cases of Jewish children disappearing into missions, where they were converted against their parents' will.

"Mr. Al-Tiri would not give up. He kept hammering on the gates of the orphanage, pleading and demanding, 'Give me back my son!' More than once the guards fell on him and beat him brutally. Then he was imprisoned on false charges in a dark cell, without daylight, for many months. When he was finally released, the sudden brilliance of the sunlight blinded him. Even then he did not give in. He contacted various influential people, but the missionary orphanage refused to divulge where the child was. They denied everything.

"Many years have passed, but The Al-Tiris still hope and pray. Maybe one day their son will come back to them, with *Hashem*'s help. Well, that's the story," she said, looking at her watch. "Goodbye, girls. I must go now."

The twosome was stunned by this tale of grief and sadness. They could imagine only a little of the pain that the Al-Tiris must be suffering. Tzivia pictured the empty rooms of their home that must have once echoed with peals of childish laughter, to be replaced with their unanswered cries of pain. Oh, what aching hearts and yearning *Tefillos*. "*Hashem*, please, please send our child back to us!"

"Two broken hearts!" Zisy sighed.

Tzivia walked slowly up her grandfather's garden path, deep in thought. Then, "Zisy, what are we going to do to find him?"

"Find whom?"

"Yosef, of course."

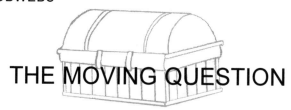

THE MOVING QUESTION

That afternoon, Tzivia visited her grandfather.

Eyes luminous with unshed tears, she followed her father into the quiet ward, her heart thudding loudly. How would her grandfather be feeling? What would he look like? She choked down a lump in her throat, and found that she was trembling.

A nurse stood at each patient's bedside. The curtains were drawn around one person's bed, but she caught a glimpse of doctors and nurses crowding around. Some machine was beeping urgently.

Zeyde lay in a bed in the corner of the ward, totally still, his face chalk-white. A tube protruded from his mouth, resting on his limp gray beard. He was connected to an intravenous drip and wires. With her eyes, she traced the wires to a machine in which there was a black balloon expanding and contracting. What monstrous machine was this? Why was there a computer screen above Zeyde's head with constantly changing numbers?

Bewildered and numb, she could only stare from the immobile invalid to the frightening machine and back again.

Mrs. Ullman put an arm across her daughter's shoulders. "Zeyde's unconscious," she explained. "This machine is doing his breathing for him and helping his heart to work. Those numbers you see on the screen are the rate of his heartbeat."

"But... But...." Tzivia stammered. "He looks terrible, as if, as if he's going to d.d.d... *Chas vesholom!*"

"Shhhh!" her mother glanced anxiously at the bed. "When someone is unconscious, they say, the hearing is the first of the senses to return. Be careful how you speak." The steady hissing and blipp-blipp of monitors and sundry machines working in the IC Unit scared Tzivia.

Rabbi Ullman said gravely, "We hope he'll recover, with *Hashem*'s help. It's up to us now, with *Tehillim* and *Tzedoka* and blessings from *Rebbeim* and *Gedolim*."

The plump blonde nurse who had been hovering at Mr. Levy's bedside gestured to Mrs. Ullman. "The medical consultant has arrived, Dearie. He would like a word with you both in the conference room. Perhaps your daughter would like to stay here during the meeting."

Tzivia's parents followed the nurse's directions to the conference room and left the Intensive Care Unit. Tzivia was left with the plump nurse and her grandfather. She kept on glancing at the still, silent figure, normally so full of life.

The nurse checked his pulse and adjusted the drip. "Listen Dearie, don't take it too hard. You can save the situation with your prayers. That's the truth, Dearie. Don't look so surprised. I am a gentile, but I do believe in the power of prayer. In fact, once, a few of my fellow nurses decided to try an experiment. There were a certain amount of mortally ill patients in the ICU. We prayed for the survival of half of them. Believe it or not, Dearie, almost all of those for whom we prayed, recovered. So keep praying.

"Do speak to your Grandpa, Dearie. He may be sleeping, but he just might be able to hear you. You can just ignore me. That's right; pretend I'm not here, Dearie. Go on, talk to him."

Self consciously, Tzivia moved right next to her Zeyde. *Tehillim* poured from her lips. She *davened*, quietly at first, and then louder.

"Zeyde," she placed her lips close to his ears. "I was told that you can hear me, Zeyde. We need you. We miss you. Come home, Zeyde. Please wake up. Speak to me, Zeyde." Her eyes were riveted to his face. There was no response.

She swallowed a sob and continued. "*Ribono Shel Olam.* Here's an *Erliche Yid.* He is totally devoted to *Torah* and *Mitzvos.* Every *Mitzva* he does is full of joy and enthusiasm. Every spare minute of his time is used to learn *Torah.* We need him, *Ribono Shel Olam*! Please let Zeyde wake up. Let him get back to normal quickly. I beg You, *Hashem*!

"Zeyde, you'll be happy to hear that I have taken on a new *Mitzva* and I've asked my friends in Preston to do the same. This should be a merit for you for a speedy recovery. You know you always wanted me to slow down my *Brochos* and think about what I was saying — to thank *Hashem* properly for my food and good health?

"Well, I've started learning the *Halochos* of *Brochos* and things have changed. *Asher Yotzar* takes me twenty seconds nowadays instead of ten! I pray that *Hashem* will restore your body to the best of health."

Was that a flicker of movement? Oh! Zeyde's mouth was

curving in a slight smile.

"Zeyde?" she asked, hesitantly.

His eyelids fluttered. His eyes opened for a moment and then closed again.

"ZEYDE!" she screamed.

The plump nurse jumped. "What happened?"

"Shhhh! You're disturbing the other patients!" an angry male nurse reproved her.

"He – he opened his eyes!" Tzivia pointed a shaking finger.

Several nurses crowded round the bed. Zeyde's eyes opened again briefly, unfocused. They shut. A doctor in a white coat ordered Tzivia to wait outside the ward and a nurse drew the curtain around the bed.

Tzivia waited obediently in the hallway outside the ICU, with no recollection of having walked there. She felt like a mound of jelly. Where were her parents? She needed them desperately now.

A Jewish woman whom she had never met before stopped beside her. "Are you okay?" she asked. "You look like you're trembling."

"I'm dazed. My Zeyde's just woken up from a coma," Tzivia responded like a robot. Her knees felt like they were buckling.

The kind stranger guided her to a bench in the corridor. "I'm so happy for you. *Boruch Hashem*!"

Tzivia found herself telling the woman all about her plea to *Hashem* and the words she had spoken to her grandfather only moments before. "I'm sorry, I don't want to keep you; you must be on your way to visit someone?"

"Yes. I visit all the Jewish hospital patients here, every Tuesday afternoon."

The teenager was impressed. "It must mean so much to lonely patients to know that someone cares enough to visit them. Maybe one day I will visit hospital patients, too. Ah, here come my parents!"

Rabbi and Mrs. Ullman were running toward the ICU in undignified haste. Tzivia ran after them. "Tutty! Mummy! Zeyde woke up!"

Mrs. Ullman turned and embraced her daughter emotionally. "Yes, *Boruch Hashem*! We found out when they beeped the consultant during our meeting! We came immediately. *Hashem* is so *good* to us!"

****

Tzivia wrote carefully, pausing now and again to think. She frowned and wrote furiously, words tumbling from her pen; then she slowed down, and finally stopped. A smile broke out on her features like the sun chasing away the clouds after a storm.

"That should be eye-catching, if only he'll read it. Hmmm. I'd better change that word." She crossed out a word and added two more. She read it through again. Yes, this was sure to attract some attention.

The text read as follows: YOSEF, YOUR FAMILY IS LOOKING FOR YOU. IF YOU WERE ORIGINALLY FROM YEMEN AND WERE ADOPTED IN GREECE ABOUT 20 YEARS AGO, PLEASE CONTACT FAMILY ULLMAN IN THE UK. TEL: 0208 800 2030. ADDRESS: 42 WATERGARDEN LANE, LONDON E5.

Tossing away all the unsuitable rough texts she had written, she indulged in some daydreaming as she packed away her pencil-case. The advertisement she had just composed would be translated into Greek by a translator and placed in prominent Greek newspapers. Yosef would hopefully see it and start thinking and remembering. Within a few weeks he would be together with his parents. She could not wait! That would be a wonderful gift to present to her Zeyde at the *Seudas Hodoa* (thanksgiving party) her parents were talking about making in gratitude for Zeyde's gradual recovery.

Which reminded her - when were they going home? Her parents had not yet spoken about traveling back home. School was to start in a few days. She had better raise the subject at supper. Who would take care of Zeyde once they were gone, she wondered. Her mother was his only child, and she had been born after seventeen years of marriage.

Although an only child, Mrs. Ullman had been brought

up unspoiled. "No fuss or feathers," her grandmother had termed her method of education. "The main thing are the *Midos*, not the type of clothes she wears. Of course, good *heimishe, Yiddishe* friends are essential. That's why we moved to Stamford Hill, even though we had a flourishing business in Sheffield," her grandmother had explained to Tzivia more than once.

Mrs. Levy had died six years ago, but Tzivia still felt a pang when she recalled her grandmother.

Slam! Rabbi Ullman had arrived. Tzivia skipped downstairs humming a tune.

Rabbi Ullman was beaming. "Mummy! Tzivia! I have the most marvelous news to tell you! *Yeshivas Chasdei Hashem* has offered me a job as a *Maggid Shiur* for 14-year olds. What do you think?"

"That's wonderful! *Boruch Hashem*! It's the answer to our prayers. Then we can move to London after all!" Mrs. Ullman's face glowed with joy. "When do you start?"

"As soon as I can. I will have to wind up my job in Preston first. The *shul* there will have to advertise for a new *Rav*."

Tzivia grimaced, her mouth wide open in surprise. "Can someone tell me what's going on?"

Her mother, looking happier than she had for ages, was enthusiastic. "We're moving to London, dear!"

"London? LONDON? Whatever for?"

"To be near Zeyde. To take care of him," Rabbi Ullman stated. "Your mother and I have been discussing this matter ever since we arrived here and found Zeyde in hospital. Secondly, but at least as important, we want to make the move for your good."

"But... but... London? What about school? I can't just stop in the middle! What about my friends? I can't manage without Charlotte Weiss! And the story I wrote for the school-magazine - what will happen to that? You don't mean this seriously, do you? It's all a *Purim* joke, Tutty? Mummy?" She looked hopefully from one to the other, but they both shook their heads.

Tears sprang to Tzivia's eyes. "You're only thinking about Zeyde! What about me?" It occurred to her that she was being selfish, but it was too late; the words were out.

The tension was broken by the peal of the doorbell. Glad to escape from the harsh words she had spoken, Tzivia opened the door to the newcomer. Mrs. Tohani, the Pakistani neighbor, stood almost hidden behind a large bouquet of flowers. "This is for your grand-daddy, from my husband and me. Is Mrs. Rabbi in?"

Mrs. Ullman bustled out to the hallway. "How sweet of you, Mrs. Tohani."

"How is the old gentleman?"

"He's progressing well, thank G-d. He'll be happy with

your flowers."

"You know, Mrs. Rabbi, I 'specially bought the bouquet from a Jewish florist, 'cos I know you keep kosher."

"Thanks again. I'll put them straight into his room for him." Mrs. Tohani departed, and Mrs. Ullman went off to hunt up a vase.

Rabbi Ullman turned to Tzivia. "Put on your coat. We're going for a walk."

Tzivia buttoned her coat apprehensively. Father and daughter walked into the rain-washed street. A few withered leaves lay limply underfoot, reflecting her low mood. She felt as if her feelings were being trodden on like the sodden leaves. Nobody had asked for or cared about her opinion in the matter. Then Tutty spoke.

"I'd like you to give your reasons for not wanting to leave Preston."

Tzivia pondered. "It's leaving school - starting off in a new place. Uprooting. Breaking up old friendships. I'm doing very well in most subjects – it would be a shame to mix it all up in a new school. As for the school magazine - they depend on me for stories. How can I let them down?

"I don't understand, Tutty. How can you be so ready to give up your job and move to Stamford Hill? What's the great deal here? Nor do I grasp how Mummy can let you. Doesn't she like being the *rebbetzin* in Preston's shul? Aren't you both doing so much for the people there?"

Rabbi Ullman paused in mid-stride. "Well, some of your points are valid and others are not. As far as school is concerned, you can make new friends and do just as well in a new school as you do in Preston Jewish High. You do not realize how vital it is for you to have Orthodox Jewish friends, in whose homes you can visit and eat. In Preston there is not even a single home whose *kashrus* we trust. And what about the televisions, books, and magazines in the homes of your classmates? Still worse, lately the Internet has gained popularity among your friends."

"What's wrong with the Internet, Tutty?"

Rabbi Ullman used his thumb for greater emphasis, as he did when learning *Gemoro* with his students. "The Internet pours dirty and immoral ideas into the mind. It destroys the holiness of the *Yid*. How can you be protected from these gentile influences, if you are visiting homes where they are welcome? It is time that we moved to a community where your friends may be even more Orthodox than you are yourself. You can only improve from having such classmates."

"And my stories for the school magazine?"

"That is unfortunate. I'm sorry, but it cannot be helped. As far as my job as Rabbi in Preston is concerned, well, nobody is indispensable. The community will be able to replace me quite easily. I have been there for thirteen years, during which time Mummy and I have helped a lot of people strengthen their *Torah* and *Mitzva* observance. Now we feel that it is time for a change.

"I have always wanted to give *Shiur* in a Yeshiva, in the

true world of Torah. Mummy, who is an *Aishes Chayil,* a good wife, wants what I want. Furthermore, Mummy would very much like to look after Zeyde. He's getting older and will need greater care after this heart attack. Besides which, lately he's been writing letters to us in Preston about how lonely he is. He misses you, too. You are his only grandchild. Mummy feels she owes it to him to move to London and make his old age as pleasant as possible."

Raindrops pattered gently onto father and daughter. Tzivia felt ashamed of her selfishness compared to the self-sacrifice of her parents. Tears trickled down her cheeks. She hoped her father would think the teardrops were just raindrops.

"I'm - I'm sorry for only thinking about myself, Tutty. It's the shock, you see. I'll have to digest the idea. You always tell me I need to put myself into other people's places to be able to understand them. I'll try to accept the idea of moving to London."

Her father nodded approvingly, and they headed back to Zeyde's house - their future home.

CHOCOLATE HOUSE

Two days after the miraculous awakening, Tzivia accompanied her mother to the hospital to visit her grandfather. He was now in a private room off a general ward.

Her grandfather's beloved face was pale. His black *peyos*, now dull and lackluster, escaped from beneath his velvet *kappel*. His silvery-gray beard moved in time to the rhythm of his sleeping form. It was wonderful to see him again devoid of tubes. Only a glucose drip was still attached to his arm.

He sighed and opened his eyes. Leaping to her feet, Tzivia exclaimed, "Zeyde, *Boruch Rofei Cholim*!"

"Good morning, Tutty," Mrs. Ullman greeted her father respectfully.

Mr. Levy smiled weakly. A lump caught in Tzivia's throat. This frail figure was but a shadow of her Zeyde. "How are you, Zeyde?"

"*Boruch Hashem*," he replied in a whisper.

"Does it hurt a lot?" was the next question.

"I have my four pills, so most times it barely hurts," the old man seemed exhausted from the effort of speaking.

"I use your four pills too," Tzivia said, eagerly.

"1) *Boruch Hashem* it is not worse,

2) *Boruch Hashem* it has not happened until now.

3) *Boruch Hashem* that besides this everything is fine, and

4) *Boruch Hashem, Gam Zu Letovah*; this too is for the best."

Zeyde drowsed again. Mother and daughter sat in silence, gazing at him lovingly. When he awoke and fixed his eyes again on his family, Tzivia said, hesitantly, "Zeyde, er... um... I found an old letter of yours in your attic at home... about how you rescued those children and lost Yosef..."

Her grandfather whispered something. She leaned over him to hear his words. "Strange that you should find that letter after all these years," he said. Her grandfather's eyes closed. She longed to pose more questions, but the rhythmic rise and fall of his chest showed that her Zeyde was asleep.

A short while later, he opened his eyes again, and the little twinkle was back. "Did a little bird whisper to me that you're working on your *Brochos*?"

Tzivia jumped up eagerly. "Zeyde, I'm really trying. I read through one *Halocha* a day! Just listen." She rattled off her newfound knowledge. "To say a *Brocha* one must have clean hands and an empty mouth. One may only say *Hashem*'s name if one doesn't need to use the bathroom, nor may one say a *Brocha* if there are bad odors within range. When making a *Brocha* on food, one has to hold it in one's right hand, unless one is a 'lefty,' in which case he must hold it in his left hand. One has to know which *Brocha* one plans to make on the food. Every word must be uttered slowly, with *kavona* (intention), and one must hear oneself saying the words. Also, one must not do any activity while saying the *Brocha*."

The old man smiled contentedly and dozed off.

Mrs. Ullman arose, placed a finger to her lips and tiptoed to the door with Tzivia. "You have to know when an ill person needs to rest. It's no *Mitzva* of *Bikur Cholim* to stay and stay when the patient prefers to sleep. A short visit is just right," her mother stated, firmly. "You go home now and eat lunch with the Drovitches. I'll stay."

A short time later, the Drovitches were sharing their lunch with Tzivia.

"I could not sleep last night," declared Zisy, depositing her empty plate and cutlery into the sink.

"Neither could I!" said Mrs. Drovitch. "Someone put the baby to bed with a wet nappy on, and he was screeching to be changed in the wee hours of the morning! But why couldn't *you* sleep, Zisy? Is something bothering you?" Her mother adjusted her apron and pulled Gavrielli over to the sink to wash his sticky hands and face.

"Yes. I could not stop thinking about that poor boy's kidnapping. He must be an adult by now, come to think of it. Stuck between non-Jews, without *Torah*, without *Shabbos*, without any *Mitzvos*. I felt so sorry for him that I couldn't fall asleep."

Tzivia helped herself to a portion of apple pie. "Did you *daven* for him? Knowing you, you probably did!"

Zisy answered forcefully. "Obviously! I said, 'Ribono

Shel Olam, please save Yosef. Please bring him back to *Yiddishkeit*; to become a *Torah*-observant Jew'. And I said, '*Tatte*, *helf* – let all of us be *frum* and *Yiddish* despite the tests that You put us through.'"

"Yeah," agreed Tzivia, her mouth full. "It's easy to be a good *Yid* when it's all going our way – when we have parents, siblings, money for whatever we need, a roof over our heads, etc, etc. The real test comes when these things are taken from us and we still love *Hashem* and do His will faithfully."

The children stood up respectfully as Zisy's father entered the kitchen.

"Hullo, everyone. Tzivia, it looks like a telegram has just arrived at your grandfather's house. Is anyone home to accept it?"

"No! My mother's in hospital with my Zeyde and my father hasn't arrived home yet!" She started out the door, and then stopped. "I haven't said my *Brocha Acharona* yet!"

Zisy ran to the door, calling behind her for Tzivia to stay and say her *Brocha Acharona* with *kavona*. Then she raced outside to intercept the deliveryman, who was already climbing back onto his motorbike. Family Drovitch watched from the doorstep as, after a few words of explanation, the motorcyclist handed Zisy the telegram, and roared away.

Zisy gave the telegram to Tzivia, who had attempted to finish her *Brocha* with *kavona*. Tzivia glanced at the telegram, and was suddenly very excited. "LOOK AT THIS!" she squealed. The Drovitches spilt out onto the street trying to peer over her shoulder, all at the same time. Tzivia read out the telegram:

I YOSEF.STOP. I COME ENGLAND 15$^{TH.}$ STOP. TELL MY FAMILY. STOP.

****

Tzivia folded the last serviette and surveyed the table. A tray of mouth-watering cakes lay on the lace tablecloth. An open carton of pure juice was sandwiched between a bottle of seltzer and some cups. "Looks quite nice," she thought. "Hope they like it."

She heard Zisy in the hallway. "Hi, Zisy," she called, as her friend entered the apartment, "I'm in the dining-room." Zisy pushed open the door and held it open with one leg for three-year old Gavrielli, who had come along. She set down a magnificent cake.

"Wowee!" Tzvia gasped. "It's a chocolate house on a layer of coconut green grass. Look at that - the fence is made of tiny wafers and it's a licorice roof! And you've put three figures at the door to symbolize Yosef and his parents! Zisy, it's smashing!"

"Thanks. It took a long time to make and this little boy here kept trying to sample some of the chocolate. Hmm, he still is, I see. Keep off, Gavrielli!"

Mrs. Ullman admired the cake, too, as she placed a bowl of sugared fruits in the center of the table. "I hope the Al-Tiris will enjoy this mini-kiddush, and Yosef too."

"When is he arriving, Mrs. Ullman?" asked Zisy, producing a pack of photographs from her pocket.

"Any moment now. My husband should be arriving back from work shortly, too. Once Yosef is here, we will call the Al-Tiris."

Tzivia pounced on the photos. "You look smashing, Zisy. Come upstairs and let's look at these." The two disappeared, and Mrs. Ullman started slicing up a batch of mushrooms in the kitchen.

Gavrielli was left alone and unnoticed in the dining room. Eyes gleaming, he drew near to the tempting array on the table. "Mmmm, drum-balls, grum-balls!" he mumbled as he stuffed his mouth with a rum ball. His little fingers helped themselves to a couple more of the cakes.

He would try some of his sister's chocolate house, he finally decided. Really, it had been very mean of her not to let him taste any of that yummy chocolate cake. Gavrielli tried, but could not reach it. It was too far in to the center of the table. Should he pull the tablecloth toward him? He tugged the lacy corner. The chocolate house inched forward, and so did the orange juice. There it was now ... nearly in his grasp. One more tug and he would have it.

The drinks moved toward him. Then the orange juice wobbled, seemed to try to right itself, and finally fell over. Gavrielli yelped as the wet, sticky juice showered his face and shirt liberally. Well, he'd make the best of it. He opened his mouth wide and allowed the orange juice that streamed steadily off the table to rinse away some bits of cake. Tiring of this uncomfortable pastime, he licked up some juice from a puddle on the table, washed his sticky fingers in it, as well, and reset the carton right side up on the table.

"Drrring!" The doorbell! There was no time to lose! He must help himself to the chocolate house as soon as possible!

Mrs. Ullman walked to the front door and admitted a thin, slight man with dark hair and brown eyes. He was carrying an overnight bag. He gave her an uncertain smile. "You put advertisement in newspaper?"

"Yes. So you are Yosef? *Sholom Aleichem*! Welcome! Please take a seat in the dining room over there and I will put on the kettle. What would you like to drink?"

"Russian tea, please, if you have."

"Certainly!" Mrs. Ullman bustled about in the kitchen while the guest carefully sat down in the dining room. The two girls settled on the stairs and viewed the proceedings through the banisters. They could catch only a glimpse of a brown head above the armchair and a side view of the table.

Tzivia gasped.

Zisy craned forward. "What's up? Can you see him?"

"No, but I can see something else that I'd rather not see!"

"What?"

"Change places with me and you'll see what I see!" Tzivia swapped places with her friend.

Zisy was treated to a bird's-eye view of the tablecloth slowly moving forward in the grasp of a chubby hand. "Whaaat? Gavrielli! No! Stop!"

But it was too late. CRASH went the cake! SPLASH went the remainder of the orange juice! A startled cry from Gavrielli and one from Yosef, as well, added to the mayhem.

The visitor jumped up. A generous dousing of juice had drenched his jacket. He lifted the half-fallen tablecloth and looked underneath. Gavrielli stared at him, frightened. Dumbstruck, the two girls watched the stranger throw back his head and burst into peals of laughter.

Mrs. Ullman chose this moment to make her entrance with a glass of black tea. She stopped short in dismay, almost spilling the drink on herself. "Gavrielli!" she exclaimed, putting down the tea. "That was very, very naughty! You'd better not stay in here, Mr... er... Mr?"

"Just call me Yosef."

"I'm terribly sorry. I see you've gotten wet."

"I no mind. Sweet boy!" Yosef chuckled and followed Mrs. Ullman into the kitchen.

A few moments later, smothered shrieks were heard from the scene of the crime. Gavrielli was crying, Zisy was shouting, and Tzivia was trying to comfort her. "*Gam Zu Letova. Boruch Hashem* that it's not any worse."

"But it *is* worse!" Zisy stamped her foot. "What more could go wrong with our lovely party?"

She was wrong. Something could be a lot worse, as she was soon to find out. The girls grimly set about clearing up. Gavrielli crept under the table and sobbed.

Rabbi Ullman walked in cheerfully, just at this juncture. He glanced at the table and then, seeing the ruins of the mini-*Kiddush*, looked again – more fixedly this time. He lifted the sodden tablecloth and then hastily let go of it after it dripped down onto his shiny shoes. Raising a drier section, he peeked underneath at the little boy sobbing there. "Why are you crying, Gavrielli?"

"Cos I want 'tention!" was the hiccupping retort.

"Tutty! Tutty! Yosef's arrived. He's in the kitchen," came Tzivia's voice.

"Good. Cheer up, Gavrielli. Here, have a rum ball." Gavrielli hid under the table again, clutching his prize to his chest, and Rabbi Ullman went to welcome his guest.

The girls passed him on their way out of the dining room with the ruined cake and empty carton of juice. After they cleared up the mess, they tiptoed outside the kitchen to hear the conversation. The stranger spoke in a heavily accented English. "Yes, is true, I born in Yemen but I live all life in Greece."

Rabbi Ullman sipped his drink. "So, you're the boy my

father-in-law almost rescued from the orphanage."

"Orphage? What? My English not good. What orphage?"

"A children's home - for children with no parents."

"No. I never in orphage. My parents die when I small - only four. The Arab sheikh, he gives me to non-Jewish parents. They adopt me, and we come to Greece twenty years. I very happy that you find my family. You find my aunt, cousin? Where are they?"

"Er... um. Can we clear up something first?" Rabbi Ullman was uncharacteristically stammering. "Did you say that you have never been to any orphanage? Could you have forgotten it, somehow? And how old did you say you were, when you were adopted?"

"No. I never go to orpha-nage, I tell you. When my parents die, the Arab sheikh, he gives me to adopt to people."

"You say your parents died. And you never went to an orphanage," Rabbi Ullman repeated, slowly.

"Something wrong?" Yosef glanced at him, anxiously.

Rabbi Ullman scratched his beard, at a loss for words. Then, "I'm afraid this will come as a shock to you. I think you are not the Yosef we are seeking."

"Not the Y... not the... What you mean?" the man said, hoarsely.

"The Yosef we want differs from you in several ways. First of all, his parents are still alive. Also, missionaries kidnapped him at the age of six. He spent more than half a year in an orphanage, and pleaded with visitors to return him to his parents. Yosef was then taken to Greece and adopted there. Tell me, are you or are you not that Yosef?"

The man put his head in his hands. "No. No. That not me." He groaned. Everyone's heart went out to him.

Mrs. Ullman spoke sympathetically. "I'm really sorry you came all the way here from Greece only to be disappointed. We would have investigated and discussed it with you in greater detail before you arrived, but you left no address or telephone number on the telegram you sent."

The "wrong" Yosef covered his face. "I so happy to think I see my aunt or cousin again! I sure they put advertisement in Greek newspapers. And most of all, I want learning about Judaism. I know nothing and want learning about *Torah*."

"Maybe I can help you there," Rabbi Ullman sat up eagerly. "I have a friend that has a *Yeshiva* for newcomers to Judaism. I am sure that he would be happy for you to join him."

The two girls listening outside the kitchen stared at each other. "A false alarm, that's all it was!" Zisy whispered to her friend. "Poor thing! What a disappointment! How is your mother going to break the news to Mrs. Al-Tiri?"

"And you thought that nothing could be worse than your cake being spoiled by Gavrielli!"

"Oy, Gavrielli! Where's that imp got to, now? He's being too quiet." Zisy charged back into the dining room. It was empty. She peered under the fresh tablecloth that she and Tzivia had spread out onto the table.

There was Gavrielli - fast asleep!

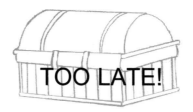

TOO LATE!

Tzivia fluffed up her grandfather's cushions as she chatted to him about this and that. Her grandfather's health was gradually improving. Today, he had color in his cheeks and was sitting up in bed listening to his granddaughter, while one hand lay on a *Sefer Tehillim*.

Suddenly his granddaughter straightened up, with a cushion in her hand and her eyes staring at a point millions of miles away. Her train of thought had shifted to a more serious subject, one that still made her feel sad. "Zeyde, I do wish we could have found Yosef. I was so hoping we would discover him before his parents go back to *Eretz Yisrael*."

"I say *Tehillim* for him every day, my child. Perhaps he'll still turn up." Mr. Levy held up the *Sefer Tehillim*.

"I give *Tzedoka* every day, as well."

"We cannot do more than that, can we?" Mr. Levy watched his granddaughter set out his medicines for the afternoon.

"But Zeyde," Tzivia faltered. "What if... what if he never does turn up?"

Mr. Levy lay back against his cushions. "We don't know what *Hashem*'s plans are, but we do know that all *Hashem* does is for the best - understand it or not."

Tzivia thought back to yesterday when she and her

mother had gone to take leave of Mrs. Al-Tiri. The Teimani woman had told them of her husband's constantly recurring dream, which was born of tortured memories.

In the dream, Mr. Al-Tiri sees his wife running into the shul, her anguished scream piercing the heavens. "Yosef is missing!"

All the worshippers stand frozen. Mr. Al-Tiri leaps forward. "W-w-what? Speak!"

"Yosef is missing!" she cries.

The picture fades.

Now he is standing before his Rav, bruised and battered, his eyesight gone.

"Mori Yihye, they beat me. They tortured me for trying to get my son back. There is no longer any trace of my beloved Yosef. Please, Mori, help me!"

In his dream the elderly sage weeps with him in sympathy. There is a heavy silence. Then: "Od Yosef Chai - your son is still alive. Some day he will come back to you, with the help of Hashem."

Bittersweet feelings of joy well up in the old man, even as he sleeps.

At this point, Mr. Al-Tiri always wakes up, and knows that it has been a dream, only a dream. But he hopes with all his heart that his dream will one day be complete, and he will meet his son again.

The three of them, Mrs. Al-Tiri, Mrs. Ullman, and Tzivia had wept, sharing the grief of a mother for her missing child and a wife for her broken husband.

"Ya Rabbuna, irhamna!" (Please, *Hashem*, have mercy on us!) was Mrs. Al-Tiri's cry. Would her hopes ever come to reality? Would she ever see her son again? Would father, mother, and son reunite to form a complete family, as they had been so many years before? Bitter thoughts swept across Mrs. Al-Tiri's heart. *"Ya Rabbuna irhamna!"* she cried again, in a hoarse whisper. She must force herself to remember the *Rav*'s promise, she told the Ullmans. She must continue to bear her lot with trust and faith in *Hashem*. He alone could and would certainly help them. *"Ya Rabbuna irhamna!"* she sighed again. "Listen to a mother's tears. The *Moshiach* will come when the ocean of tears in Heaven are full. Please add mine and hasten his coming," she murmured in Arabic. She had fallen on Mrs. Ullman's neck and wept. Tzivia heart hurt as she felt this woman's pain, which had not diminished, even after so many years.

Tzivia jerked back to the present as a door slammed. She heard voices murmuring excitedly downstairs. Then footsteps raced up to them, and her father burst into the room. She had never seen her father quite so excited. "Zeyde, you'll never guess what's happened!" he cried out.

"Tell me," Mr. Levy became tense.

"Yosef! I think I've found Yosef!" Rabbi Ullman whispered.

Tzivia let out a whoop of joy. Her grandfather began to breathe heavily. Her father rushed over to him and felt his pulse. "I'm sorry for shocking you like that!"

"I'm all right," the old man said, his knuckles tensed white around the *Tehillim*. "Where is he? Are you sure this time?"

"Well, not one hundred percent; not yet. But if this is the right Yosef, then he's right here in England! Read this!" Rabbi Ullman dropped the copy of the *Jewish Times* onto the bedside table.

Mr. Levy shook his head. "I'm not up to reading yet. Could you?"

In a breathless tone, Rabbi Ullman read the article. Tzivia's eyes were drawn to the headline: "JEW OR GENTILE? *Last week, the celebrated architect, Theo Constantinou, discovered, after 30 years as a gentile, that he is actually a Jew! Theo, who has lived in Greece for many years, has designed many buildings across Europe.*

Snatched from his Jewish family at a tender age, Theo was adopted by a Greek couple, who gave him a loving upbringing and excellent education. Ignorant of his true Jewish heritage, he has lived a secular lifestyle for over thirty years.

He told our reporter: "I have had plenty of money and fame during my architectural career but very little true satisfaction. I always felt that something major was missing from my life. I'm going to check into this Judaism thing to see what it has to offer me. I've lived a lie all my life! It is time that I found out the truth!"

Constantinou has no idea as to where his birth parents are at present. He would welcome any information. A reward is being offered to anyone who can help him discover his Jewish birth parents or other family members. Please call the following telephone number.

Mr. Levy's brow puckered in amazement. "It's a London phone number. Have you called yet?"

Rabbi Ullman shook his head. "I'm about to do that now."

Tzivia tensed as she heard the dial tone. Could this really be Yosef? Would it be another false alarm? Her father spoke into the receiver.

"Hello. Am I speaking to Mr. Theo Constantinou?" A pause.

"Good. My name is Rabbi Ullman, calling from here in London. I'm phoning in connection with the newspaper article in today's *Jewish Times*."

"Yes, I do have some information. But please tell me – when you were born? Thirty-seven years ago? Hmmmm. That fits. Do you happen to know in which country you were born? YEMEN?"

There was pin-drop silence in the room. They could hear a torrent of excited words through the telephone wires.

Rabbi Ullman was nodding silently and smiling, his face shining. "We think you may be the child of Teimani parents, kidnapped at the age of seven... You were hidden in a monastery... Do you remember anything about priests? You don't?"

Tzivia whispered urgently, "Ask him if he remembers Thomas at the orphanage?"

"Thomas at the orphanage. Do you recall such a person?" They could hear words pouring forth from the receiver.

"That's right...It's coming back to you now? Well, of course, we cannot be sure until you meet them... You see, we've had one false alarm already; we must be cautious. Yes, it's possible, though... This is just unbelievable! Where are you?" A pause. "How long would it take you to get here? Okay, this is my address. See you soon, please G-d." Rabbi Ullman replaced the receiver with a broad grin. "He'll be here in twenty minutes."

The tall man who walked in closely resembled Mrs. Al-Tiri. Dark-skinned, with black, soulful eyes, he looked around eagerly at the assembled group.

Mr. Levy and his son-in-law welcomed him warmly and ushered him to a chair. He spoke English with a Greek accent. "Please tell me about the people you think are my parents."

Rabbi Ullman related what he knew about the Al-Tiris. Mr. Levy regarded him searchingly. "If not for the fact that you look very much like Mrs. Al-Tiri, I would easily have mistaken you for a gentile."

A deep flush spread over the architect's cheeks. "I always thought I was non-Jewish too, until last week. Do I really look like my mother – I mean, Mrs. Al-Tiri? You see, my real name is Al-Tiri. I was able to find out that much. I did not include it in the newspaper article because I did not want any fakers or con artists, to pretend to be my family. You know, for the reward."

Tzivia gasped to hear that his name was Al-Tiri, but she kept quiet. "Will you share your story with us?" Rabbi Ullman beamed at their guest. Mr. Levy's eyes sparkled with excitement and constrained joy.

"Up until several years ago," began the man with a far-away look in his eyes, "I lived in Greece. I had a good education. Graduated from school with flying colors. Did very well in university. I spent several years studying architecture in London and obtained a topnotch position here in England. Now I have my own company. I have been successful, thank G-d, but I've always known that there is more to life than that. But I was, until recently, far too busy to start searching for that something I knew was missing in my life."

His audience listened with bated breath.

"Last week my mother – or shall I say my adoptive mother – became mortally ill. My parents – er, my adoptive parents sent for me to take a leave of absence and come to see her. Back in Greece, I was shocked at the change in her. She looked like a living skeleton. 'Father' would not leave her alone for a moment, so I did not have much of a chance for a heart-to-heart talk with her. However, the day finally came when he had an important appointment. He left me alone with Mother for a few hours, and gave me strict instructions regarding her care.

"I think that this was actually the first time that Mother and I had been alone in quite a few years. 'Son', she said hoarsely, 'come closer. I've got to tell you something important before I die.' She gasped for breath. 'Your father never let me tell you this, but...' she wheezed and then choked on a racking cough, 'now he's not here. I've got to relieve my conscience before I die.'

"'Don't speak like that, Mother. You've still many long years ahead of you, I hope,' I tried to soothe her.

"She shook her head impatiently. 'I know I don't have much longer to live, my son.' Her eyes wild, her face alternately red and then pale, she pointed a finger at me. 'You - you are a Jew! Your name is Yosef Al-Tiri!' Her breath became even more labored now. 'The orphanage near Yemen gave you to us at the age of seven. We had been childless for many years and we paid them well for a child.'

"I was stunned. My whole world had turned upside down in an instant. 'You mean, you - I'm not your son?' I asked her.

"She nodded weakly, and I could see a nerve pounding at her temple. 'Forgive me for not....' she said hoarsely, 'for not telling you all these years... your father would not allow it.'

"Suddenly, she stretched out her arms - and then it was all over. 'Mother! Mother!' I cried, but it was too late.

"My father returned to find his wife dead. After we had wept for some time and then calmed ourselves, I asked him pointblank. 'Father, I'm Jewish, aren't I?'

"'Whoever told you such nonsense?' he scowled.

"'Mother revealed it to me a few moments before her death. She told me you'd never let her tell me the truth. Don't lie to me, father. I am Jewish, aren't I?' I asked.

"He admitted it, sobbing brokenly. That was how I found out only last week that my entire life had been a lie. I begged this man who had acted as my father to tell me about my real parents.

"He confessed. 'You came to us at the age of seven. In the beginning you refused to eat anything - you said you would only eat kosher, as Jews do. And you kept trying to cover your head even though we constantly removed your head covering. You used to murmur your Jewish prayers, too, until I finally managed to get you to church and you learned our prayers instead.

"'You were a hard nut to crack!' he said. 'But I was determined not to allow a little lad of seven to beat me! The nightmares you had! You woke up in the middle of the night, shrieking and clutching the sides of your head. 'Don't cut them off!' you screamed. 'Abba! Ima!' you cried out. Mother would take you in her arms and whisper sweet nothings to you until you calmed down. You melted our hearts, even as you tried so

73

hard to defy us.

"'But a child needs love and a home, and so, eventually, you forgot your past. You settled down and we were the best parents anyone could have wished for. Weren't we?' he seemed to plead.

"'Father, you gave me everything,' I told him. (Everything but Judaism, I thought.) 'I will always be grateful to you both. But father, if my real name is Yosef Al-Tiri, where are my real parents? Are they alive? Al-Tiri does not sound at all Greek.'

"He replied, 'I don't know, son – can I still call you that? The orphanage refused to pass on any details. The person who brought you to us allowed us to persuade him (with a fat bribe) to reveal your name, and that you originally came from Yemen. But more than that I don't know. I can hunt up the orphanage's name and telephone-number, although they might have changed after all these years.'"

Theo Constantinou/Yosef Al-Tiri clasped his hands together in a gesture of wonder. "A week ago I never knew anything about my true birthparents," he said. "Now I have the chance to meet them!"

Mr. Levy put a hand out to the younger man. "I have the address of the orphanage. You could take the orphanage to court for kidnap and unlawful adoption procedures."

Yosef sighed. "I have already looked into that. The orphanage closed down over fifteen years ago and the Father in charge has since died. A few monks who worked there have left the country, probably to evade arrest. I had to come back to

England in the meantime, back to my job. I had decided to hire a private detective to trace my parents, but thanks to the news article, I've met you, and now that will not be necessary." He paused and took a deep breath. "One more question: Are my parents still alive?"

All eyes were now riveted on Rabbi Ullman. He stroked his beard. "The Almighty directed our steps to meet you. And what's more, we know where your parents are. They have been in England for two months now, for medical treatment for your father. In fact, they are neighbors of ours. What's more, they will be traveling back to Israel any day now."

The architect jumped up. "Take me to them!" he cried out. The note of longing in his voice brought tears to Tzivia's eyes.

She cleared her throat. This was not going to be an easy bombshell to drop. "I'm sorry, Tutty, but the Al-Tiris left England this morning. They've returned to *Eretz Yisrael* um... to Israel."

"Whaaaat?" the architect paled. "I've just missed them?"

Rabbi Ullman patted the despairing Yosef on the shoulder, as the man held onto the handrail of Mr. Levy's bed to steady himself. "Gone! They've gone! Do you have their address or phone number in Israel? No? Last week I thought I had Greek parents! This week I know I have Yemenite parents who have just returned to Israel! When will I have the privilege of seeing them in the flesh?"

Mr. Levy beckoned to the despondent architect and

began to talk to him about trust in *Hashem*. Rabbi Ullman motioned to Tzivia to answer the door.

She felt drained from the drama of the past half-hour. How would it all end? She opened the door wide. Zisy stood there wearing her usual endearing grin.

"Hello, stranger. Haven't seen you yet this afternoon. Did you hear the latest news?" Zisy's face became serious.

Tzivia glanced at her friend. She had news for *her*, as well.

"I can see you're just dying to know," Zisy said, dryly. "Well, you know that the Al-Tiri's were supposed to leave for *Eretz Yisrael* this morning?"

"Yes." Tzivia perked up. That's what all the trouble is about, she mused.

"Well, it seems that just as the taxi arrived to take them to the airport, Mr. Al-Tiri had a heart-attack. He ended up going to hospital by ambulance, instead. Hey, Tzivia! Where are you going? Why are you running up the stairs? Why are you shouting, 'They're here!' Who's here? Tzivia? Tzivia?"

FINALE

"Straight train to Preston," a metallic voice announced. Tzivia glowered at her reflection in the window, wishing she had boarded the wrong train. She frowned at the ticket collector, and sulked.

Diamond-like raindrops spattered against the windowpanes. The train sped past industrial factories that belched out their dirty smoke. Villages, towns, and fields raced past. It became difficult to see out, for darkness had long since fallen.

It was *Motzoei Shabbos*. Rabbi Ullman and his daughter were traveling up to Preston for a few days to pack up the house and choose what to leave behind and what to send on to London. They also needed to make the house presentable for prospective buyers. Several people had already expressed interest in the house, and they had hired a real estate agent to take care of the sale.

Tzivia was confused. Did she want to move? She wasn't really sure, but a large part of her felt as if she was being forced into a step that would affect her whole life.

Tzivia reached for the window beside her, slid it upward as far as it would go, and poked out her head. The cool spring night was exhilarating. The wind whipped her hair back. Lights twinkled at her from darkened towns. The sound of the train flying along the tracks was deafening. Suddenly, the branches of a tree reached out to scratch her. She drew back her head, closed the window, and pressed her face to the glass.

A *Seudas Hodoa* had been made for both Zeyde and Mr. Al-Tiri only that week. Amidst friends and neighbors, Zeyde had sat beaming at the dais together with the newly reunited father and son. It had been an emotional occasion. Yosef had tapped a bottle with a spoon to quiet those assembled, and then stood up to speak.

"Thank you, thank you everyone. It's wonderful to be part of the Jewish Nation again. All these years I felt that something was missing from my life, and I already feel a tremendous sense of satisfaction from the very small amount of Torah that I have begun to study. Mr. Levy, we have discussed how you once tried to restore me to my parents. I thank you and your family for doing so now, after all these years. And most of all, I thank the Al-mighty for His kindness to me. Thank G-d, my father's apparent heart-attack was only a strong attack of arthritis, which prevented him from moving. As you can see for yourselves, he is now much better." Mr. Al-Tiri had nodded and smiled in his wheelchair, exuding contentment. He understood little of the English, but he proudly listened to his newly restored son.

On the women's side, Mrs. Al-Tiri was positively glowing with joy. Her lips whispered words of thanks and praise to *Hashem* for all His kindness to her family.

Mrs. Ullman clapped and wiped her eyes surreptitiously. She had outdone herself in preparing a scrumptious meal for the occasion. The table was bedecked with a large bouquet of flowers, courtesy of Mrs. Tohani, and Zisy's new, unspoiled chocolate house was the attractive centerpiece of the *Seudas Hodoa*.

"Speech, Mr. Levy! Speech!" Mr. Drovitch had

demanded, banging on the table for silence.

Zeyde sat up a little straighter, combed his beard with his gnarled fingers, and spoke quietly. People respectfully leaned forward to listen. "With praise and thanks to *Hakodosh Boruch Hu,* I am alive and well. With my four pills," he winked at Tzivia here, "I survived what might have been a fatal heart attack. I want to thank my son-in-law, daughter, and granddaughter for nursing me so devotedly back to health. The many chapters of *Tehillim* that were said for my recovery were surely a great merit for me, and also for other Jews that are sick. I'd like to thank my grandchild Tzivia, who asked her class in Preston to commit each week to strengthening a particular *Mitzva.* I feel sure that the merit of all those *Mitzvos* speeded my recovery."

Applause greeted his speech. When it had petered out, Rabbi Ullman took over. "Zeyde, we have a special gift for you tonight. You haven't seen the back of us, yet. We are moving to London to stay with you."

There were gasps of surprise and admiration. Mr. Levy's eyes widened. A joyous smile stretched across his lips. He stared at his son-in-law. "You really mean it?"

"Would I tell a lie?"

People crowded round to congratulate Mr. Levy and to shake Rabbi Ullman's hand. A joyous "*Lechayim!*" was drunk and the men and boys danced around and around to a happy song. Eventually all the guests reluctantly took their leave, to the sound of good wishes.

The Al-Tiri's were the last to go, promising to return for another visit before leaving together to *Eretz Yisroel.* At the door, Yosef clasped Rabbi Ullman's hands warmly. "I can never thank you and your family enough."

"We'll be in touch, *Im Yirtze Hashem. Kol Tuv.*" Rabbi Ullman escorted the happy family down the path.

After everyone had departed, Mrs. Ullman wished her father a personal *lechayim*. "To a good life and to peace," he echoed. "I don't know how to thank you sufficiently. You are actually moving here to live with me! Oh, what *Naches*! *Lechayim*, Tzivia!"

Tzivia reluctantly raised her little goblet of grape juice. She could not respond very enthusiastically, but she did not want to mar her grandfather's happiness. She wished that she could be happier about moving to London! Luckily, at that moment, the phone rang. "A well-wisher for Zeyde," Mrs. Ullman announced.

Now Tzivia and her father were going back to Preston to close up the house and sell the home she had known for so many years. She would be giving up her friends, her school, and her normal daily life as the Rabbi's daughter. She wallowed in self-pity.

"We shall be arriving in Preston shortly," the metallic voice announced. "Kindly check that you have all your belongings with you before you disembark."

They lined up with the other passengers near the train exits, barely able to make out the yards of railway tracks that the train was traversing. Here was Preston, at last.

The station was pulsating with life, despite the lateness of the hour. Porters drove trolleys of cases along; people rushed hither and thither. Relatives hugged each other. Whistles shrieked. A train chugged away.

A short time later, Father and daughter arrived at their darkened home, each thinking very different thoughts. It was cold and cheerless inside. Being unoccupied for several weeks had caused the house to smell musty.

They switched on the lights and the heating. Their *Melave Malka* consisted of *Challah* that they had transported from London and a tin of sardines.

Tzivia *benched* quietly, and then sighed a deep sigh. Her father regarded her sternly. "Tzivia, stop feeling sorry for yourself," he said. "*Hashem* gives everyone trials and difficulties in life. He also equips us with the ability to successfully overcome them. Some people have serious illnesses, poverty, unhappy marriages, or quarrels with others, etcetera. If your trial is merely to accept that you have to move to London, you have to thank *Hashem* a million times, and more, that it's no worse than that. We all experience situations that we do not enjoy, but we have to learn to accept them. As one great man said: 'If this is Your will, *Hashem*, then it is my will, too.' Hmmm... Why don't you try to use Zeyde's four pills?"

Tzivia had to smile at that. Then she became serious again. "I can try," she said.
"Good girl," said Tutty. "Now, let's go to bed; it's late."

The next morning Tzivia awoke refreshed from a

surprisingly dreamless sleep. After washing *Negel Vasser*, davening, and eating an apple she found left over in the refrigerator, she hurried to her room. There was a lot to be done.

She started by sorting out the cupboards in her room. Hoards of notebooks from her school years stood in a pile on the dresser. Should she throw them out or not? She opened one and read, "Reb Bunim of P'shischa stated: 'It is a wonderful S*egula* in all spiritual and material matters, both great and small, to pray to *Hashem*.'" The book continued to lie on the dresser as she pondered the message.

"*Tatte* in *Shamayim, helf mir*," she spoke to *Hashem*. "Help me find the right attitude to be content in London, and be happy and make my parents happy."

Just then, the front door slammed. Her father had arrived home from *Shacharis*, his *Tefillin* bag and some groceries in his arms. As they ate some sandwiches, they were suddenly disturbed by the tramp of many feet and conversation in their front garden.

"Tutty," she gasped as she peeped through the dining room curtain. "There are loads of people coming to our door!"

"Don't worry, Tzivia. Just carry on with your breakfast." He went to admit the crowd of men from the community, who had come to visit their Rabbi. "Gentlemen, to what do I owe the honor of this visit?"
A voice, which Tzivia recognized as belonging to Mr. Fryden, the president of their shul, boomed, "Good morning, Rabbi Ullman. We are here to tell you that we cannot accept

your resignation! What will we do without you?"

There were murmurs of agreement. Someone shouted, "We'll increase your salary! Please don't leave us, Rabbi."

Another man, Mr. Barr, protested, "If the Rabbi wants to quit, he surely has good reason for doing so. Let's listen." He was immediately shouted down.

"Gentlemen," Rabbi Ullman excused himself. "If you will come into my dining room, we can discuss this matter calmly. Please, allow me to *bentch* first. I just finished my breakfast." Rabbi Ullman resumed his place in the kitchen and recited *Birkas Hamozon* unhurriedly and carefully. His daughter marveled at her father's sincere prayer, knowing the pressure he must be under. After he finished, he took a bottle of soda water and some tumblers, and disappeared into the dining room.

Tzivia felt a trace of unease. The men seemed very determined to keep her father as Rabbi of the *shul*. Perhaps they would persuade him to stay after all. Well, that was what she wanted, wasn't it? Suddenly she was not quite sure.

Raised voices came to Tzivia from the other room. She tried to hear, but only caught random words being tossed about: "Double your salary!" "Car!" "Vacation!" Mostly it was just mumble, mumble. Feeling edgy, she began packing the kitchen towels into an empty tangerine crate. Yes, they would end up staying in Preston. She would not have to leave school after all. They would convince Tutty.

Then she thought about her mother. She would surely be bitterly disappointed. Mrs. Ullman desperately longed to look after her father in his old age. One night, Tzivia had awoken to hear her mother downstairs making a hot water bottle for her grandfather. Tzivia had padded downstairs in her slippers. "Mummy, it's the middle of the night! Aren't you exhausted?" Mummy had smiled. "Isn't it too hard for you to cope with Zeyde?" Tzivia had burst out, knotting the belt on her robe.

Her mother had filled the hot water bottle with water from the kettle. Then she answered, "It may be difficult at times, but I owe my father so much. Together with my mother, he brought me up, clothed me, fed me, and gave me love and nurturing all my life, providing me with all I needed. They did their very best, and more, for me.

"The least I can do now is look after my father and make his last years pleasant. The A-lmighty will give me the strength and willpower to manage. May He assist me to honor and respect Zeyde for as long as possible."

Mr. Levy had also felt so much better since they had told him that they were there to stay. Maybe, after all, she herself did want to move to London.

"Wonderful! Smashing!" boomed Mr. Fryden from the other room, awakening Tzivia from her reverie. Then, more mumble mumble. She couldn't hear the rest. How frustrating! But Mr. Fryden must have meant that Tutty was agreeing to stay in Preston after all. Oh no! She didn't want that anymore! Now that she was beginning to like the idea of moving to Stamford Hill, the decision had been turned around. Tzivia shook her head. What irony!

Why had Tutty gone back on his word? He had seemed thrilled with the idea of becoming a lecturer in the yeshiva in

London. Yet, now he was about to give up all his plans for an increase in salary? Where were his noble principles? She longed to run into the dining room and scream her disagreement. Instead, she stayed in the kitchen, biting her lip and wringing a dishtowel.

No! She would not let it happen! She could not! She would call her mother in London and get her to dissuade her husband. She scaled the stairs and rushed to the upstairs telephone extension. She yanked the receiver off the base and pointed her finger to dial, then stopped short. The telephone was in use.

Her father was saying, "...make the members of our shul very happy." The receiver slipped from her hand and crashed to the ground. It was settled then. They would remain in Preston. The thought made her miserable. The tears dripped onto her lap.

Time crawled as Tzivia waited for the guests to leave. At last the house emptied out with a final chorus of "Goodbye, Rabbi," "See you at *Mincha*," and, "Thanks for your time."

A footstep sounded on the staircase. Rabbi Ullman's eyebrows were raised quizzically. "I thought you'd have finished at least one room by now. Why are you slumped on this chair?"

Tzivia said sluggishly, "What's the point of packing if we're not moving?"

"Well, *I'm* moving; I don't know about you."

"What? But... but... your salary and... you agreed!"

Her father sat down and regarded her with a twinkle in his eye. "Tut! Tut! Eavesdroppers hear very little truth! You heard a few extracts of the conversation and put two and two together. Only this time you made five! Here's what really happened, Tzivia. I told my congregation that I knew of just the man to take over for me as Rabbi. He's been *Rav* in a small community in Scotland for several years. Have you ever heard of Rabbi Reuven Hess? Everyone agreed that he would be the right candidate for the post. I phoned him to offer him the position, at double the salary that he's getting at present. He happily and quickly accepted the position. He will be arriving in a couple of days for me to show him around. Then he'll take over my job here."

Tzivia jumped up, half laughing and half crying. She wasn't sure whether to faint or to dance around the room. "You mean we're going to move to Stamford Hill after all?"

Rabbi Ullman nodded vigorously. "We'd better get cracking with our packing. You do this room and I'll start on the *Seforim*."

The next day, as Tzivia set to work on her parents' room, she came across an old trunk under the bed. The trunk had been there ever since she could remember and she had never looked inside. Would she find another mystery letter? She curiously lifted the rusty lock and opened the lid. Inside lay a set of *Shabbos* clothes, neatly folded. The clothes obviously belonged to her father.

"Tutty, can we throw out that old trunk in your room? We can hang your extra *Shabbos* clothes in a wardrobe instead."

"Oh, no. That's my *Moshiach* trunk. I inherited it from my father. When I hear *Moshiach* arrive, I'll quickly put on my *Shabbos* clothes and run out to greet him. If *Moshiach* hasn't come by then, we'll be on our way back to Stamford Hill. That trunk must travel with us. But let's hope we'll be traveling with *Moshiach* to *Eretz Yisrael* instead, in the very near future!"

GLOSSARY

Asher Yotzar	Blessing said on leaving the bathroom
Bentch (Yiddish)	(to say the) Grace After Meals
Bikur Cholim	Visiting the sick
Birkas Hamazon	Grace after Meals
Bood (Yiddish)	Bath
Boruch Rofei Cholim	Blessed is He who heals
Brocha Acharona	Blessing said after eating
Brocha/Brochos	Blessing(s)
Bubbele (Yiddish)	Term of endearment, lit., little grandmother
Chas Vesholom	It should never happen
Chazal	Our great men of blessed memory
Daven (Yiddish)	Pray
Eretz Yisroel	Israel
Erliche (Yiddish)	Fine/Religious
Farshtei (Yiddish)	Understand
Frum (Yiddish)	Religious
Gantze leben (Yiddish)	Whole life
Gedolim	Sages/Great people
Hakadosh Boruch Hu	The Holy One, Blessed Be He
Halbe (Yiddish)	Half
Halochos	Laws
Hartz (Yiddish)	Heart
Hatzolah	Jewish volunteer First-Aid Emergency-Response

Heimishe (Yiddish)	Literally: like at home; warm
Helf (Yiddish)	Help
Im Yirtze Hashem	If G-d wants
Kapel (Yiddish)	Yarmulke, skullcap
Kashrus	The quality of being kosher
Kavona	Concentration
Kind (Yiddish)	Child
Kleine (Yiddish)	Small
Maggid Shiur	Teacher of a Torah lesson
Mein (Yiddish)	My
Meshuge (Yiddish)	Crazy
Midos	Qualities
Mincha	Afternoon prayer service
Mir (Yiddish)	Me
Mitzva/Mitzvos	Good deed(s)
Mori Yihye (Arabic)	Title for teacher
Od Yosef Chai	Yosef is still alive
Oy vay (Yiddish)	Oh, terrible!
Peyos	Locks of hair worn in front of a jewish boy's ears
Rav	Rabbi
Rebbeim	Teachers
Rebbetzin (Yiddish)	Rabbi's wife
Ribono Shel Olam	Master of the World
Salaam Aleikum (Arabic)	Hello
Sefer/Seforim	Book(s)
Seudas Hodoa	Feast made to thank G-d
Shabbos	Sabbath
Shacharis	Morning prayer service

Shamayim	Heaven
Sheyfele (Yiddish)	Term of endearment, lit/ Lamb
Shiur	Lesson
Sholom Aleichem	Hello to you
Shul	Synagogue
Tefilla/Tefillos	Prayer
Tefillin	Phylacteries
Tehillim	Psalms
Todah Rabbah	Thank you very much
Tzadikim	Righteous men
Tzedoka	Charity
Tzitzis	Religious fringed garment
Yid (Yiddish)	Jew
Yiddishe (Yiddish)	Jewish
Yiddishkeit (Yiddish)	Judaism
Yingel (Yiddish)	Boy